NOT DEAD YET

NOT

DE

HADLEY MOORE

AUTUMN HOUSE PRESS

and other stories

A D

YET

WINNER OF THE 2018 AUTUMN HOUSE FICTION PRIZE

Autumn House Press receives state arts funding support through a grant from the Pennsylvania Council on the Arts, a state agency funded by the Commonwealth of Pennsylvania, and the National Endowment for the Arts, a federal agency.

ISBN: 978-1-938769-41-2

Library of Congress Control Number: 2019933814

Cover photo by Marc Volk, fStop/Getty Images

Book & cover design by Joel W. Coggins

All Autumn House books are printed on acid-free paper and meet the international standards of permanent books intended for purchase by libraries.

for dusty

CONTENTS

WHEN MY FATHER WAS IN PRISON

We had this bird called Smokey that my brother taught to say *Nevermore*, but he (Smokey) couldn't ever really do it since he was the wrong kind of bird. Not a talker, my mother said.

There was a girl across the street whose father was a government functionary. My brother made me repeat the words to get the sounds right and when I asked what that was, he said it was almost the same thing as being in prison, except her father slept at home.

Two church ladies came to bring us Christmas presents. The presents were SpongeBob SquarePants pillowcases, and the cards were in my father's handwriting (how did they do that?) but you could tell the gifts weren't really from him, my brother said, because in spite of everything he wasn't that stupid.

All my brother felt about him anymore, he said, was the lack of him, and that made my mother look up from her cutting board and say, "You're getting a little too big for your britches, aren't you?" And my brother said it was true: none of his pants fit. Other kids had fathers with jobs who could buy their kids new clothes, even the girl across the street's father, and you know what he was.

I heard my mother on the phone saying, "I think the boys will kill me. That's what I really can't stand, not the—" And then she walked away with the phone, and I didn't know what wouldn't kill her, but I knew my brother and I might.

I opened my brother's door without knocking, and his friend Carl was kneeling on the floor and my brother was sitting on the bed. I shut the door right away and blinked and blinked, but I could still see them without their pants on and my brother's hand in Carl's red hair and Carl's face somewhere in there with the blankets and my brother's legs.

My brother told me later it was just something you did when you were fifteen, but he wouldn't look at me for three days, and I wanted (but also didn't want) to ask him where were their pants? What had happened to Carl's face? I counted the years from nine to fifteen, even though I knew how many it was, and six seemed like a lot but also not enough.

Smokey died and we put him in a cereal box, which seemed like the wrong kind of box because even though he went right in, there was a lot of space left, so my brother stuffed in the SpongeBob pillowcases and closed the box and then wrapped it in flowered paper like it was a present, which actually it (the pillowcases) had been in the first place. *Ashes to ashes*, my brother said. *Circle of life*.

We went outside to bury the present under the pine tree in the backyard, but we had to wait until almost dark because this was a rented house. The landlady might not want us digging holes, my mother said. *Nevermore*, my brother said.

My mother took me to a church that had something called prison ministry, but my brother wouldn't come and the church was just regular anyway. No one said anything about prison or asked us about my father. When we got back, my brother and Carl were sitting on the couch watching SpongeBob. My brother had a pillow on his lap and was holding the remote, and Carl's face was red like his hair. I'd heard a new word at school, so I tried it. "Hey, dicksucks," I said, and my mother swatted my butt and my brother said, "Idiot," and Carl just got redder and stared at the TV and blinked and blinked, like how I'd blinked after I shut the door on them.

He (my father) sent us letters. "Hey fellas! How's my boys? Your pops is okay. We got to watch a movie the other day—The Great Escape. Ha ha just kidding. Actually it was a movie about penguins. You know I'm helping out in the kitchen here. It's not too bad for a job. Well do good in school and be nice to your mom—don't give her any hassles, and I'll see you soon okay? Your dad loves you. P.S. Sorry about all this."

My mother let me keep the letters in a drawer in my room. First she would read them and then I would read them and then my brother would read them, and then he'd give them back to me and I'd put them in the drawer. But once—it was after Smokey died—I showed my brother a letter and he blew his nose in it and crumpled it up and dropped it on the floor. He didn't even read it. "Nevermore," I said, and he laughed, and then I said, "Dicksuck," and he punched me in the head.

The girl across the street and her father waved to each other every morning, and he beeped his car horn, and when the weather got nice the girl would come outside and wave from the front porch. She'd wave until his car turned at the end of the street. I watched her while I ate my english muffin before school and practiced saying *government functionary*, but when I actually said it to her—I opened the front door and yelled it this one time—I got mixed up and said, "Your dad is a government dictionary!" Then I slammed the door and opened it again and screamed, "Dick! Suck! Your dad is a government dicksuck! Dicksucktionary!"

I got in trouble and before school the next day we had to go across the street so I could apologize. "Sorry," I said to the girl and her parents. The girl was a grade younger than me and I wondered if she'd ever heard *dicksuck* before. *Dicksucktionary*, I thought. "I'm sorry," my mother said. "I'm not sure where he got such a filthy word." *Go look it up in the dicksucktionary.* I had to squeeze my lips together not to laugh, and I looked at the girl's father and he was squeezing his lips together too. When he saw me looking at him he covered his mouth and coughed. "Boys, you know," he said.

My mother took me back to church and this time she asked a lady about prison ministry and the lady said hang on and came back with a brochure. My mother looked at it and said, "Oh, it's for when they get out." The lady nodded and said, "Do you know someone who could use it?" and my mother said, "Maybe." Then it seemed like she tried to smile a little and almost couldn't. "But it won't be for a while."

Carl was over all the time during the summer and I knew to leave him and my brother alone. Sometimes they watched TV and sometimes they sat outside and sometimes Carl stayed for dinner when my mother got home from work, but mostly they were in my brother's room with the door closed doing what you did when you were fifteen.

My brother was supposed to be watching me, but I drew pictures of Smokey and my father and SpongeBob by myself, and I looked out the front window for the girl across the street and her father, and I went out to the pine tree in the back where Smokey was buried. I tried to pray there, by Smokey's grave, but I ended up just saying *prison ministry* and *nevermore* and sometimes *government functionary* over and over. I tried not to say *dicksuck* too much.

Carl and my brother were in my brother's room, and then they came out and my brother was following Carl saying, "Hang on, wait just a minute. Carl, please. Just—stop for a minute." But Carl walked past where I was, at the kitchen table drawing the girl across the street's father, and his (Carl's) eyes were open really wide and his mouth was a straight line. I put my head down and they passed me and went outside and then my brother came back and his eyes were open really wide and his mouth was open too and he sucked in air like he couldn't breathe, and he wouldn't look at me. He passed me going the other way, and I said, "Boys, you know." He stopped like he was waiting for me to say something else but I didn't know what else so I just put my hand out, the hand with the pencil, but my brother couldn't see because his back was to me, and then he kept going, to his room again, and he slammed the door and stayed there doing whatever it was you did when you were fifteen and all by yourself.

One of the things you did when you were nine and all by yourself was look in the drawer full of letters. The letters were folded up except for the one my brother blew his nose in. I uncrumpled that letter and scratched the dried snot off, and it was the same as all the others so it didn't matter that my brother hadn't read it. My father was okay, he loved us, he was sorry. Except in this one he spelled "sorry" "sory," and I thought, *My father needs a dicksucktionary*. This seemed like something my brother would maybe think was funny, but since Carl left—when was that? like a week ago?—my brother hadn't thought anything was funny at all.

I heard my mother on the phone again saying we would kill her and that my brother was hormonal or something and I had a mouth on me. *Dicksuck*, for Christ's sake. Where did I get this stuff? I was *nine*. When she hung up I shouted from the other room, "Boys, you know?" She was quiet and then she said, "You got big ears, kid." And then, "Do I ever know."

My brother didn't want to go back to school to start tenth grade and I told my mother it was because of Carl. They had a fight. So? my mother said. Friends fight. They'll get over it. He has to go to school. To my brother: You have to go to school. Just tell Carl you're sorry. I am sorry! my brother yelled. He's (Carl's) not sorry! He doesn't care! And he (my brother) started sobbing and slammed the door of his room and then kicked through it so we could see his shoe sticking out a little before he pulled it back in. Hey, I said, this is a rented house, and my mother held one hand out and shook her head at me to be quiet, and she put the other hand over her mouth but I could still hear her say, *Ohhhhh*. Oh Jesus. Ohhhhh, Jesus. Oh. Oh. Oh. Jee*esus*.

We were getting ready to visit him (my father), but my brother wouldn't go and my mother cried and my brother told her he was unmoved and she couldn't physically get him in the car, he'd like to see her try. My mother said she didn't know when else we'd be able to go and my brother said he didn't care, he really really didn't. So my mother put her head in her hands and my brother said, "Just don't tell him about Carl, okay?" And my mother said, "Oh honey. Jesus." And she picked her head up and touched my brother's knee and he took her hand and put his arm around her and they sat like that for longer than I could watch them doing it.

My mother and I drove a long way and when we got there I didn't want to get out of the car. She said it was get out by myself or she'd pull me out and carry me in, I was small enough and she was big enough. So I got out but then I threw up. It was a surprise throw-up, and I didn't think I was really sick but I was kind of glad I did it.

We walked to this place where my mother had to take her keys and her coins out of her pockets and I asked if I could keep the quarters when she got them back, and she said this really wasn't the time and the man who took her stuff and locked it up winked at me.

Another man came and we followed him to this room that looked a little like school, and then two other men brought my father in. I almost threw up again but I didn't, and he (my father) sat down at the table in the middle of the room with my mother and I stood there for a minute and then I started walking. I went around the room a few times, and my father said, "C'mere buddy" and asked how old was I these days, but that seemed like something he should have known so I didn't answer. "Nine," my mother said. "Almost ten," I said. "Almost ten," my father said, and I looked at him, all the way around him while I walked, and he looked different but I wasn't sure exactly how. "So what's going on with your brother?" my father asked. "What's he up to?" I looked at him and I looked at the men who'd brought him in—guards—and I looked at my mother, who seemed very ugly all of a sudden, and I said, "I don't know, probably dicksucking." One of the guards sort of laughed, and the other one said, "Hey kid, don't talk like that," and I shrugged and thought *boys, you know* and kept walking. My mother and father didn't say anything and my father probably just thought I was kidding. "Anyway," I said, "he didn't want to come and see you."

My mother pretty much didn't say anything in the car on the way back, but when we got home I was grounded. I wasn't allowed to play outside or see my friends, but I also decided not to watch TV or look in the drawer of letters for a whole week. Mostly what I did was come home from school and lie on my bed. Once in a while my brother would look in at me and ask, "Still wearing the hair shirt?" and I didn't know what that meant but I didn't want to say so. I wished he'd come inside and ask me about prison. But when he finally did I didn't answer. So he sat on the floor and after a minute he said, "Wanna name people we don't like?" We used to do that at family reunions when my mother made us go, before Grandma and Grandpa died. So in my room after I visited my father in prison, we named Uncle Rob and two of our cousins and some kids from school—tenth-graders he knew and fourth-graders I knew; we took turns—and then we were quiet, thinking up other people we didn't like, and I said, "Carl?" and my brother coughed and said, "Yeah. We don't like Carl." We were quiet again and after a while he said, "Dad," and I said, "Yeah, Dad. We don't like Dad. That dicksuck." And my brother didn't say anything, but he laughed, which meant he finally thought it (dicksuck) was funny.

I turned ten, and my brother turned sixteen. Our birthdays are close together—October 28, November 12—and we got cards from prison and my father didn't say anything about how I visited him there. They were just normal birthday cards and said the normal things, and my brother read mine when it came and then he read his. He didn't blow his nose in them, and I put them in the drawer and that was it for our first prison birthdays even though my mother tried to act excited for a while, but I think we were all glad when it was November 13 and she stopped.

After November 13 were Thanksgiving again and the day my father left again and Christmas again and after that I'd forgotten but it was the day Smokey died again, and my brother came into my room in the morning and said *Nevermore*, and I started to cry but pretended I didn't because it was just a bird in a cereal box with SpongeBob pillowcases (the church ladies never came by for Christmas this time), and our house was just a rented house, and my brother was just a dicksuck.

I wrote it on the wall of the bathroom at school the day Smokey died (again): dicksuck. But they knew it was me, and when my mother got there she said, "This is really your calling card, huh?" and she went in the principal's office and I sat outside the door for a long time and when she came out she didn't seem as mad as I thought she'd be. So I asked if she was mad and she said yes and later when we got home she said, "I'm tired of this. Okay? I'm very very tired of it. It's time to stop now. Will you just stop?"

I said I would stop but I had to go to the school counselor anyway, two days a week during lunch. The counselor let me eat while she said she imagined things were difficult and confusing for me right now and was there anything I wanted to talk about? My father, maybe? Or anything else? I thought for a minute, and then I asked her, "Will I get in trouble if I don't know what to say?" and she said no, so I didn't say anything and she let me sit and eat and look out the window until lunchtime was over. Before I left I thought I should tell her something so I said, "My bird died. His name was Smokey." She nodded and said, "I'm sorry that happened," and I nodded back, because I was sorry too.

I told my brother the school counselor asked if there was anything I wanted to talk about and he said he hated that question because how could you even start? Yeah, I said, but I like her anyway. Does she have big boobs? my brother asked and I tried to punch him but he grabbed my wrist and I said do you even like girls? He dropped me then and I finished the punch. Do you think Dad will be mad if he finds out? I asked, and my brother said he would be long gone before Dad got out so it hardly mattered. He'd be in college, he said. He'd be an adult. Hell, I'd be an adult. It was going to be a long time. *Nevermore*, he said.

It was winter still but we had a sort of nice day, and after school I played outside for a while and the girl across the street's father came home and he waved to me. I waved back. He said, "Nice day, huh, kiddo?" I nodded and watched him climb the stairs and he was wearing a shirt and pants and a tie. When he opened his front door I yelled, "My bird died!" but he must not have heard because he went inside and didn't look at me again.

I went inside too. My brother was there in the living room and he said don't do that and I said "What?" And my brother said don't solicit attention like that, like you're the poor little boy without a father. "What?" I said. And why are you so hung up on that stupid bird? my brother said. It's more than a year since he died and you didn't even care about him then. "What?" I said again. "What? What?" Listen, my brother said, I'm serious. It just makes you look pathetic. No one cares about Smokey. You don't care about Smokey. "What?" I said, really loud now. God! my brother screamed. I fucking hate this! "What?" I asked, for real this time. "What do you hate?" You! my brother yelled. Everything! All of this!

There was a lot of stuff to hate. That was what I said to the school counselor, after a few times of sitting in her office eating my lunch. "Really?" she said. "Like what?" Like getting in trouble, I said, and having your bird die and your brother yelling at you and your mother saying you might kill her. Stuff like that. Plus living across the street from a government functionary. "Hmm," the school counselor said. "Anything else?" Lots else, I told her. *Lots* else. Lots. I mean *lots*.

A new boy (James) started coming around with my brother. On the phone my mother said, "Honestly, do you believe this? At least no one can get pregnant. Jesus. There better be a special place for me in heaven when this is all over, no kidding."

My brother wrote an essay for school about how his father was in prison and the teacher gave him an A and asked if he would want to publish it in the school paper. No, my mother said when he told us. I'm not asking you, my brother said. Honey, it's a really good essay, my mother told him. I'm so proud of you. But please don't do this to our family. Everyone knows already, my brother said. You're a fool if you don't realize that. My mother started to cry. But you have no right to tell people all about us. This is my story, my brother said. I have a right to my own story.

I told that to the counselor the next time I saw her. "I have a right to my own story." She nodded and said that was certainly true. We didn't talk for a minute. "I told you Smokey died," I said. Yes, she said. I looked out the window and there was snow still but not so much anymore and I said, "That happened when my father was in prison, all of that." I looked at her and she was looking at me. "He just. . . died. Smokey. I kind of can't believe it." That is hard to believe, she said. It really is a strange, hard thing. "He's in prison now. Still. My father." She nodded again and asked, How do you feel about that? "I don't know," I said, and I breathed out hard. "I mean, I'm just saying, is all," I told her. "I'm just telling you what happened."

THE ENTOMOLOGIST

Earlier today the hippies had ambushed Lynette, and in the hours since they left she'd been off-kilter, lost in a vacant sort of perseverating that came down to feeling humiliated and not knowing how to soothe herself.

She guessed the hippies had tried the broken bell first. Then they knocked while she was in the bathroom, and she'd hoped she could hold her breath and wait them out. But they knocked again. She debated whether to flush, decided against it, and crept from the back of the house up the hall, at the end of which she saw a man's face pressed to the wide front window. He waved. She considered running out the back, but he might chase her. She couldn't remember if she'd locked the front door, and it seemed safest to meet him on the porch where the neighbors could hear her scream.

She opened the door. "Yes?" she said.

There were two of them, the man and a woman. They were skinny as new trees, and though their clothes were shapeless, they had bathed and combed their hair. Portland was lousy with vagrant youths—"hippies" was probably an old-fashioned word—but these two appeared neither sinister nor pathetic. Even so, Lynette reminded herself to keep her guard up.

"Yes?" she said again.

"I'm Antoine," the man said.

Lynette crossed her arms.

"And I'm Catty," said the woman.

"Catty?" Lynette repeated.

The woman smiled. "It's a nickname that stuck."

The man went on, "Like Antoine de Saint-Exupéry."

"Huh," Lynette said. She pulled the door shut behind her and took a step forward. Antoine and Catty took a step back.

"We're from Oregon Micro Farms," Antoine said. "Have you heard of it?"

Lynette stared at him.

"We notice you have a chunk of unused land—"

"What?"

"Behind the house."

"You mean my yard?"

"It's a full quarter acre, and it's mostly empty."

There was a toolshed she hadn't unlocked in years and a dying crabapple tree.

"What do you want?" Lynette asked. She tried to sound impatient but the sun lit Antoine's white-blond hair. "You have a halo," she told him.

"Excuse me?"

"Oh, not a halo—a, like, nimbus or something. Of light." Lynette drew an imaginary circle around the top of her head and pointed behind them. They looked.

"The house faces west," she said. "So, your hair." It was four o'clock on a March day in Portland.

"Oh," Catty said. Her hair was black.

Antoine touched his head. He and Catty glanced at each other.

"You must have lovely sunsets," he said.

"The backyard faces east, which would give us enough light, and we could use this south-facing side yard too." Catty pointed.

They talked, and Lynette watched their mouths. Antoine's head still blazed, and the colors in their clothes pulsed, first the orange flowers of Catty's floppy sweater, then the blue-blue of Antoine's jeans. Lynette felt heat begin in her solar plexus. She wiped her upper lip.

"*Something, something,* Oregon Micro Farms," they said. "*Something, something, something,* vegetables. *Something, something,* raised beds." That phrase over and over—raised beds.

"I'm Lynette."

They stopped talking.

"Anyway," Antoine said. "Can we show you what we mean?"

That was how she ended up in the backyard with the hippies, all three of them assuming the posture of the surveyor: wide stance, hands on hips. Antoine and Catty would build raised beds on her "land"—they would start tomorrow—and maybe also plant a few hardy fruit trees. Some of the food they would donate to shelters and soup kitchens, and some they would sell at farmers' markets to benefit Oregon Micro Farms. They would get to keep a little for themselves—it was part of the contract—and they would give a little bit to Lynette.

"I'm allergic to cucumbers."

"Got it," said Catty.

"Is this your job?" Lynette asked.

"Partly. I nanny, and Antoine works in a coffee shop."

"Everyone in Portland works in a coffee shop." Lynette laughed. "Of course, I love coffee."

Antoine smoothed his beard. It was darker than his hair.

"What do you do?" he asked.

"I study termites. Studied them. I'm retired."

That surprised them. They thought she was a nutty old lady, but she had a master's degree in entomology.

"Interesting," Antoine said. "Studied them for what purpose? I know they're helpful for decomposition in some ecosystems."

Lynette guffawed. "Like decomposing the ecosystem of your house!"

They gave her tiny fake smiles.

"I worked for a pesticide company."

The grudging smiles persisted, but Lynette knew she had said too much. The heat began again, and she fanned her face. She was embarrassed because, for one, the hippies didn't believe in pesticides, and for two, the termites were back.

* * *

Her humiliation was like having a chocolate cake in the house. She would think about it until it was gone. She would eat the cake in anticipation of the relief of not having to look at it.

There are things everyone knows but no one recalls learning—boys and girls are different, all of us will die. Her bewildering humiliation was like that. She had always known it; it was more than familiar, it was atmospheric. She got in trouble as a child for transgressions she didn't understand she'd made. *Be friendly. Smile and say how do you do. Look at people when they talk to you. Please try to seem like you're having a nice time.* She would try, but it was hard to tell if she was doing it right.

Also atmospheric was her preference for animals, particularly insects (abundant, intricate, six-legged!) over humans. *For goodness sake, Lynette, stop digging in the dirt.* She would go along, interacting with humans, or at least being where they were—and doing what they wanted her to do; it was easier than navigating on her own. So she was bossed around on playdates, then later on dates and at parties, her looks, she would come to realize, earning her heaps more patience than if she'd been homely in addition to strange.

"You're so pretty!" girls would say, wistful-like, while the boys looked at her sidelong. This started when she was nine or ten. Then the boys got bigger and introduced her to the word *hot,* a word that could both thrill her and twist her stomach. She was tall, and very blond, and was made to understand that she was striking. But if she'd been homely people might have been more willing to leave her alone.

Now, Lynette glanced at her watch. Since the hippies left, five hours ago, she'd intended to call the dermatologist, do laundry, pay bills, give herself a cream rinse, and mollify her tenants, who were still pissed off about the mold in the shower. But all she'd done was bang around the house and check the termites about ninety-five times.

She sat at the kitchen table and kicked off her slippers. The window looking over the backyard was a black square, so she leaned to the wall and turned out the light. There was just a quarter moon, and the crabapple remained the same stark sculpture she'd stared at for more than twenty winters. Soon it would reveal whether it had survived this one. The toolshed lay outside her sightline and was not worth moving to see.

Tomorrow would begin the construction of the raised beds, large wooden boxes laid out geometrically. They were efficient and also attractive, the hippies had told her. She would like them; they would improve her property.

Lynette had made a resolution, and she reminded herself: she would not mention pesticides again. And she would not mention pests.

A couple of weeks earlier, she had met the termite evidence with acceptance. Insects outnumbered humans some 200 million to one. That a relative few should show up in her house again was not surprising, though it was ironic. Or maybe just coincidental.

She'd been vacuuming the living room—which was itself notable; usually she just ran the dustbuster around corners—when she bashed through the baseboard on a not-very-aggressive pass. She turned off the machine. On hands and knees she held her nose to the wood. It smelled moldy. She hooked a pinky finger inside the four-inch gash and drew out dirt. On each side of the gash she pressed, and on each side it gave a little.

Lynette switched on the light and sat. She fixed her eyes on the new hole, then moved them slowly up until she noticed a rippling in the wallpaper. She leaned forward and ran her hand up too, until she could no longer reach. Then she sat back. She had to check the basement.

Directly below was the furnace room, where no one had been since the igniter for the tenant unit was replaced a few years ago. But the two old furnaces had been kicking on and heating the house, and more and more it seemed better to leave well enough alone.

Descending the stairs, she was calm in anticipation of what she'd already identified. She opened the door to the furnace room, and swept her flashlight beam up and down the south wall. Then she swung to the north, and on her third pass up she found the mud tubes. They had bloomed from a crack in the foundation, four separate termite highways straining for a food source. The tubes had reached the wood of the floor joists overhead and wrapped around the cross braces like vines. She noted a pulse of pleasure in the recognition: *Reticulitermes hesperus*.

She went upstairs for her penknife and came back to slit open the base of the widest tube, revealing the tiny white workers, further evidence, wholly unnecessary. This must all be destroyed.

* * *

In the morning Catty and Antoine began hauling wood into the backyard. They parked a rusty Toyota pickup in front of the house and used the south side yard to go back and forth. Catty wore a flowy skirt like a pioneer wife, and Antoine had on overalls. Lynette watched them alternately from the bedroom and kitchen windows. They would come and go, they had told her. They wouldn't bother her. They didn't say where they would use the bathroom. Not inside the house.

Even so, she batted cobwebs out of corners, ran a wad of tissues over the lid of the toilet tank to grab the dust, gave the bowl a vigorous scrub to loosen the layer of scum that now waved in the water like a lacy sea creature. She wiped her sleeve across the mirror and gave herself a good looking-over.

Gray hair a springy cloud she could tie a knot and put a pencil in to hold it. No makeup, prominent crow's feet, and pale, shriveled lips. But eyes still bright blue, brows still dark, pores still small, chin still single.

And she wore a bra, for heaven's sake. Under a gold kente cloth tunic she'd found at Goodwill, but still, she made some effort. She sneezed into her elbow. She was nearly seventy, but she'd been attractive, arresting even, when she was younger.

Lynette opened the medicine cabinet, thinking she might find an old lipstick or blusher. She poked around for a few seconds, knocked a label-less tube of ointment into the sink, replaced it, and shut the door. She pursed her lips and pinched her cheeks and blinked several times. The color rose from her heart up across her chest and throat, seeping and uneven like something spilled. She turned from the mirror, stalked out of the bathroom, and shut the door behind her.

She sneaked back to the kitchen and leaned against the window frame, peering out at Antoine and Catty's progress. There were two small trees in plastic tubs (pears? apples?) set against the shed; ten or twelve bags of soil, or manure or peat maybe; and stacks of wood, two-by-fours or four-by-sixes or whatever, long reddish rectangles. Everything new and raw.

Antoine and Catty came around from the side yard, each carrying another load of boards. Antoine set his down next to the others, then took Catty's and set those down too. They stood for a few minutes, hands on hips, or hands pointing at things, or hands gesturing to each other. Catty looked at Antoine, and Antoine looked at Catty, and Lynette watched the swiveling of the backs of their heads, black to blond and blond to black.

They turned toward the house and shaded their eyes. Antoine held a hand up toward the window, and Lynette did not move. Then they left, back around the side yard to the front. The truck started, and she exhaled.

It was only 10 a.m. Lynette knotted up her hair and put on a sweater and went outside. The neatness of their supplies was even more impressive up close. Corners had been lined up, bags stacked like with like, three soil to every one manure and peat. The trees were indeed pears. She wondered where they had used the bathroom.

How long could this go on? They would build their raised beds and plant their trees and vegetables, and winter would come, and would they be back next spring? For years and years and years, every spring? Eventually they would realize they needed real jobs, or they would break up, or Catty would get pregnant, and the raised beds would fill with weeds and rot, and the trees with worms, and Lynette would either be dead or the one to witness the entropy.

Or the house could fall first. Not literally fall, but be eaten to crumbling. It would take a while. People thought termites worked very quickly, but that was only because by the time they discovered any damage, *Reticulitermes hesperus* had been working for years. The bugs ate from the inside out.

It was almost a decade ago that she had come upon a termite swarm in the front yard and hired her employer. But now it had been so long since her retirement, and the new owners were lying low because of all the bee deaths last summer. Anyone would have sprayed like that for aphids, but they clearly overdid it: 50,000 bees dead. Anyway, she felt awkward going back there. Maybe no one would remember her, and she wanted to do some research on her own, besides. The science would have progressed in the last half-dozen years. A few weeks would make little difference.

There had been a memorial service for those bees. Oh, Portland. Maybe Catty and Antoine had gone. Did you sing at a service for bees? Were there prayers? Lynette stared at the boards and bags and the trees in tubs and tried to imagine it. Was there a minister? Some Unitarian Universalist probably.

"Mrs. Collins?"

Lynette turned around. The tenants were striding across the lawn. "Christ," she said.

They caught up to her. "What's going on here?" That was the white fellow, Mitchell, the more obnoxious one. The other one was Prashant, who told her he was from Kerala (in southwest India—she'd had to look it up). When they moved in, seven months ago, she'd asked them, "Are you roommates?" That was an idiotic question, but what she'd meant was, Are you gay? Mormons? Adopted?

They were graduate students.

"The university's kind of a hike from Southeast, isn't it?" She'd meant Portland State, downtown. They went to Western Seminary, they told her, only a few blocks away.

"That's handy, then," she'd said.

They were neat and almost silent in their apartment, but they complained, more than any other tenants she'd had. It was mold in the shower or condensation on the insides of the windows or ants in the kitchen or noise she could hardly recall making, just the incidental sounds of daily puttering on her side of the duplex. *Her* side. It was all hers. This backyard too. She didn't have to answer to Mitchell.

"Oh, some young people are planting some things," she said to him now. "Raised beds."

"Some young people?" That was Prashant. He sounded more British than Indian.

"A couple of—" She didn't want to say *hippies*. "A couple of gardeners."

Mitchell sniffed. Prashant just looked at her.

"You rented your yard?" Prashant again.

"Yes." Should she have asked for money? The hippies were like tenants, but with no monthly rent check. So the benefit to her was what, again? Property improvement. Fruits and vegetables. "But I wonder how they knew this big yard was here," Lynette said out loud. Had they been lurking around her neighborhood? She felt hot again and shrugged her sweater off her shoulders. She sat on a pile of boards.

Mitchell started up. "Anyway, we wanted to ask you—"

"I know, the mold."

"Not the mold. We just bleached the heck out of it." He smirked. Why should he care about mold? He was transient. None of the responsibility was his.

And the bleach was supposed to bother her (no makeup, kente cloth tunic, "Keep Portland Weird" bumper sticker on her car, and now urban farming). It did not bother her. Lynette wondered what the tenants would think about a memorial service for bees. She was so hot. She wanted to put her head between her knees.

"What then?" she asked.

"Will this be loud?" Mitchell made a half-pointing, palm-up gesture toward the wood. "A lot of hammering, I mean."

"Oh Jesus," Lynette said. Now they would complain about the hippies too. She fanned her face and chest. What the hell was going on? She was well through menopause. "You could tell them when you'll be gone. You could give them your class schedule." She'd tried to sound sarcastic, but the tenants looked at each other. Prashant shrugged.

"When will they be back?"

"I don't know," Lynette said.

"What do they look like?" Mitchell asked.

"They look like hippies."

The hippies came back in the evening. No sooner had they braked in front of the house than the tenants practically galloped across the front lawn to meet them. There were handshakes all around, and the tenants gave the hippies a sheet of paper. Catty held it and Antoine looked over her shoulder, and they nodded, and the four of them laughed. Mitchell turned to indicate the house behind them, and Lynette shrank from the front window, where yesterday Antoine had pressed his face.

So they were friends now, the earnest farmers and the earnest Christians, and they had come to an understanding about how and when they would all make use of her property.

*   *   *

A month ago Lynette had let a plumber into the tenants' apartment while they were in class (rust stain, dripping tub faucet, weeks of complaints about the noise), and after showing him the bathroom, she'd walked through the other rooms. For all their fault-finding it was the first time she'd had real cause to be in Mitchell and Prashant's space longer than a few minutes, and without them present.

The apartment's familiar layout mirrored the side where she lived, kitchen and one bedroom in the back, living room and the other bedroom in the front. Bathroom between the bedrooms, where the plumber was banging away. That was some top-dollar noise he was making. It sounded a little overdramatic.

In the kitchen was a small dining table set with a laptop and a manila folder. She lifted one corner of the folder and let it drop. In the refrigerator, their food was labeled, black magic marker for Mitchell, green for Prashant. Each had his own carton of eggs. Mitchell preferred orange juice, Prashant whole milk.

Prashant had the back bedroom (she knew by the family photo), with just a twin bed, tidily tucked in with a navy blue quilt, and bookshelves made of stacked milk crates. Mitchell's front bedroom had a double bed with a yellow chenille blanket and two tall bookcases—proper bookcases, but cheaply made.

The living room held two more dining chairs and a card table on which was set up an elaborate board game printed with a map of the world. Lynette moved an olive-colored battleship from Spain to Brazil.

Were they friends before seminary, or did they get matched by some questionnaire on which they'd both indicated they were spartan housekeepers who liked war games?

"Ma'am?" the plumber called.

Lynette stepped away from the game, her face warm. This was innocent; it was hardly even snooping, and she only ever did it with the chaperoning presence of someone she'd hired.

She paid the plumber and ushered him out, and it was after she'd gone down the porch steps and across the lawn to her own porch that it occurred to her she might have looked in the bedroom closets. She hesitated at the bottom of her steps. The key was still in her hand. She made a tight fist, then pocketed it and climbed.

* * *

It was ten years ago that her husband died and left her this house and its mortgage. Her husband! Remember that little fiend? He'd insisted on buying a duplex so he could install his father on the other side, and then Lynette was the one left with the old man. God, why did anyone marry anyone?

Her father-in-law was from Mississippi, and he called her a hant, sometimes a haggard old hant, or an old gray hant, or that old hant the bug scientist. He thought that last one was a terrible insult, an aspersion on her femininity.

When her husband died, the old man told her she'd never be

able to keep up the house on her own. He wanted her to sell and give him half. When she refused he demanded she buy him out. She should kick him out, but she didn't say so. *I certainly will not* was all she told him, and after that were a few days of stand-off followed by an announcement he was leaving and she should just see if she could take care of this house by herself!

It was months later, when she was well past his whiplash-strange departure—she had her first tenants by then, it seemed like the thing to do—that she was paging through *The Oregonian* and saw his name. He'd been beaten and robbed in his apartment in Gresham, and he'd given an interview from the hospital. What he said was unmemorable, two or three quoted lines about how he never hurt nobody and you sure couldn't tell about people these days, but there was a photograph of the alleged perpetrator that stopped her.

He was an obvious meth head, a white kid, with the cratered skin and collapsing mouth, a twenty-year-old flat-faced fetal alcohol baby. You saw these kids all over. Familiar face, familiar revulsion, but a weird realization rose in Lynette: she sympathized with neither her loathsome father-in-law nor the loathsome kid who beat him. She stared at the photo and waited for some fellow-feeling for the poor old man or the boy who'd had no chance in life at all, and she thought of her husband too. Didn't he deserve compassion? (Obesity, aneurysm.)

She never saw her father-in-law again. He might be dead now. She never told anyone what happened to him, because whom would she tell? It was this secret scrap of knowledge she didn't care about, exactly, but that was hard not to be captivated by for its utter strangeness. She still carried it around with her.

Those first tenants moved out after a year. There were three of them, a couple plus a single woman, which seemed suspicious, and Lynette wasn't sorry to see them go. She kept up the house: mowed the lawn, cleaned decently, hired things done when she had to (cracked chimney, termite swarm in the yard). After a few years she retired, so she had plenty of time, but there was so much disintegration and undesirable growth and breaking apart. She was way too old for chaos to be an epiphany, but it could still stun her how just waking up in the morning or looking out the window might bring new discoveries of rot.

It was all her responsibility, and had been now for years. She wouldn't wish back her husband or his father, but living by herself, in a duplex, made her feel like everything she touched fell to shit. She reminded herself that falling to shit was the state of the world. She was a scientist. She knew about entropy.

So she took care of the house on her own. Well, so what. She knew she would. She wasn't interested in proving anyone wrong; who cared what ghosts thought? She stayed because this house was hers alone and you had to live someplace, the way you had to have a body, everything contained. It could all be such a burden.

She advertised sporadically. Tenants came and went. They finished out their year-long leases, or they didn't and she kept their deposits (she could use the money). She never took things from them; she only brushed through their lives as she let in plumbers, plasterers, electricians. The tenants asked for the essential repairs, and even then sheepishly: *the toilet won't stop running, we wake up with plaster in our hair, anything plugged into this outlet gives a shock.*

If they were home, she waited in the entryway while the broken things were fixed, magazine in hand, leaning against the wall or sitting cross-legged on the tile. Tenants might hover in the living room and ask if she wanted a chair, or retreat to a bedroom or the kitchen and keep quiet.

If they weren't home, she wandered. She touched only the things that were out, like books, things a guest might touch, but also shoes piled by the door or coupons fastened to the refrigerator or pictures hung on the walls. She would adjust several items, but each only a little.

She wanted her tenants to feel not endangered, not even haunted, really—but askew. She wanted them to know that everything here was hers, and all of it hard-won. They could come and go, and lodge themselves and their belongings with her for a little while; they just could not stay.

❊ ❊ ❊

In the morning the hippies didn't come until ten, their presence her new signal that the tenants were away, in class. Outside it was sunny, and Lynette watched Catty and Antoine in the back for a few minutes, then grabbed her keys and made her inefficient way across the front yard to the tenant unit. A portal between the living rooms would be easier.

She had been down to the basement already today, before the hippies came. By the time she'd detected them, the termites had done what they could do down there. They had reached a spectacular food source and were deep inside it, their progress undeniable but obscured, revealed only when, for example, she banged the baseboard with the vacuum sweeper. She'd been gentle with woodwork and walls since then.

But she still liked to visit the furnace room. Early in the morning, first thing, she had gone down to run her fingers over the mud, a combination of earth and feces and saliva. She had swept her flashlight up each mud tube, one by one following their paths to her floors, her walls.

It was hopeful prospecting that sent the termites up the concrete foundation; they might very well find nothing, and Lynette had to admire their single-mindedness. That admiration was an occupational hazard—intense study produced respect bordering on envy. They were only insects, but some of her colleagues could relate. How could you not sort of love the system of it, the workers, the soldiers, the reproductives, and the queen, that hyperprolific mother? Lynette's life was all happenstance—things happened to her, she endured them. But entomology she had chosen. Or, rather, she had recognized her singular interest, and followed it.

She had spent her career in the lab, removed from the dirty work, and so she could forget her purpose for weeks at a time and be lulled by pure, conceptual-seeming science. But then she would remember.

Now, she stood in the tenants' entryway and took stock. The card table was bare, the war game nowhere to be seen. She had no reason to be here. She crossed to the kitchen and glanced to see that Catty and Antoine were still occupied. They would plant the trees first apparently; they were digging holes some six or eight feet apart. She wondered when the building would begin. No loud hammering yet.

Lynette opened the refrigerator. *She had no reason to be here.* Two loaves of bread, two cartons of eggs, all labeled. Two crispers of vegetables—they must have an understanding of whose was whose. Lynette removed the eggs and set them on the counter. She opened the cartons. Prashant had four eggs left, Mitchell seven. She picked up one of Mitchell's eggs and made a fist around it. It was cold against her palm and she squeezed a bit, then deposited it in

Prashant's carton. She put both cartons back where they'd been and closed the refrigerator.

In the bathroom a red towel and a white one hung on the bar, and the medicine cabinet held the usual things—toothpaste and brush, floss, razor—two of each, but only a single box of band-aids. Perhaps those were fine to share, or someone was immune to cuts and scrapes. The bathroom didn't interest her.

In Prashant's room Lynette licked her thumb and pressed it to the face of the man she assumed was his father in the photo on the sill. The man smiled at her with his arm around her tenant.

And in Mitchell's room, she sat on the bed to put a dent in his stretched-tight covers. She preferred Prashant to Mitchell. She preferred the hippies to Mitchell. She preferred the termites. Mitchell was hard to look at, smirky and pimply and overweight. Red-haired. Pasty. He was chief complainer, and clearly the ringleader of the hippie charm offensive, printer of the class schedule, bleacher of the shower stall, and the one with the hypersensitive hearing.

She leaned over and looked under the bed. Nothing. Like Prashant, Mitchell had no bedside table or dresser. She wanted drawers in which to find porn (preferably gay) or drugs or bookie sheets. She stood and opened the closet. Inside were a hamper and tennis shoes and flip-flops on the floor, plus a dozen or so hangers with pants and shirts. Four stacked milk crates held underwear, socks, T-shirts, and sweaters, and that was all. Nothing interesting, nothing incriminating.

Lynette sat down and then lay back, her arm under her head. She put her feet flat on the bed and let her knees fall together. She might have dozed a few minutes, because when the drilling started she found herself sitting upright, her hand on her chest. "Jesus!" she said out loud. "Jesus."

She got up and crossed the hall to the kitchen. The hippies were using an electric drill, of course, not hammers. It wasn't even that loud now that she was fully awake.

Lynette went back to Mitchell's room, closed the closet door, straightened the bed, and stood before the bookcases. She found a Bible with a gold cover and moved it down one shelf, and then one more.

Sometime after lunch the hippies' drilling stopped and birdsong crowded in. Lynette got up from her couch, where she had been not reading exactly, but riffling a magazine and holding still to keep down her heart.

She stood back from the kitchen window a couple of feet. Catty and Antoine held court with Mitchell and Prashant, there on her lawn, among their planted trees and what looked like one finished box—the first raised bed—and one that was C-shaped, three quarters done.

The C-shaped thing enclosed the four of them. Her tenants smiled while the hippies talked and pointed at their bags of soil and peat and manure, their handiwork so far, their trees. They stepped outside of the C, and the tenants followed them. Antoine made broad strides across the lawn, flicking his wrist at intervals as though he held a wand that might cause the whole yard to leaf and fruit. He looped around and ended between the pear trees, grinning like he'd conjured them. He and Catty had conjured it all, the trees and boards and bags of rich material. They had conjured the lot itself, and the house, and the woman standing at the window, though they did not see her.

Perhaps she should go out and make herself visible, remind them, disturb their breezy new friendship. She could get something out of the shed or inspect the lawn for bare patches—her shed! her lawn!—and then ask them in for tea, reproach and forgive them.

Antoine put a hand around a tree, the one nearer the old crabapple. His audience joined him, and all four of them looked into its heights, just one foot above Antoine's and Prashant's heads. They stood there like worshipers, and Lynette counted to thirty before Catty stepped back, interrupting their adoration. She pointed at the crabapple, and the others nodded, and then she swept her hand in a half-circle to indicate the yard. The men laughed, and Lynette's heart bulged and twisted.

When Mitchell showed up on her porch later, Lynette squared herself for a confrontation. Sure enough, he had a complaint, but it wasn't this morning's egg or slimy thumbprint or migrating Bible. It was the window in the kitchen. It stuck.

"It's still March," Lynette reminded him. "What do you want to open the window for?"

"I like fresh air."

"Go outside." He'd just been outside. She'd seen him.

He smirked.

"Does it have to be that window? Can you open a different window?"

He shook his head.

"Bang on it. It's probably painted shut. I don't know what to tell you."

He sighed.

"Get your friends the carpenters to help you." She jerked her thumb toward the backyard. "They seem to be moving right in."

He shrugged. "You let them."

"They just appeared!"

He shook his head again and opened his mouth and closed it. "I want—" he started, and turned to look down the street. He turned back to her. "I just want to open the window." He thumbed a pimple on his chin.

"Would you like a cup of tea?" She wasn't sure whether she had any tea.

His brows came together and one side of his upper lip quivered. "No," he said. "Thank you."

"Why do you care about any of this? None of it is your problem." *Window, mold, rust, ants.* What would he do if he discovered the termites? They might swarm at any moment. "None of it is yours."

"It is mine, Mrs. Collins. It is mine for one year. That is what a lease is for."

They stared at each other. Lynette felt her nostrils flare and that roaring heat from the middle of her chest.

He went on, louder. "And it is true for Catty and Antoine too. I assume you had them sign something."

She was hot all the way through now, hot in layers: skin, muscle, bone, and organ. "For Christ's sake, wouldn't it be easier not to complain about everything?" She wanted to tell him a few things about ownership, about rot and responsibility and infestation.

"So you won't fix the window."

"No," she said. "I sure as hell won't."

After dark she went outside, and the cold of the March night was easier on her heart than the warming daytime. The moon was nearly full, and Mitchell and Prashant could look out and discover her if they wanted to. It was her yard.

The pear trees were spindly things, sticks dug into the ground, so unlike the old crabapple. Soon, if she were lucky, leaves would hide its knotted skeleton. The pears had tiny, incipient foliage, the crabapple none yet. But the crabapple was continuous with the earth, and the pears looked as though they'd breached it, the sod disturbed, the dirt swollen like blisters around their trunks. She could pull them out with her two hands.

The first two raised beds, one still unfinished, each lay beside a pear tree. She squatted to examine the unfinished bed. It was more complicated than she'd realized, with stout posts in the inside corners, to which the boards were fastened. Would the posts face into the ground, or out of it, to hold some kind of net or trellis?

Lynette stood and looked down at the structure. She touched her toe to the long end, then pulled her foot back and kicked the bottom board, heel first, with enough force to hear a snap. There was no visible crack in the wood, just some small giving-way inside, and she let that echo. She let it knock around her skull.

❊ ❊ ❊

Twenty-odd years ago she'd met her ex-husband at the bar where he worked. She liked to think of him as her ex-husband, but what he'd actually been was first her regular husband, and then her dead husband.

She had let herself be talked into going out with co-workers one Friday when, apparently, the bartender had noticed her. Her co-worker Holly, who was dating her co-worker Sean, told her.

"What?" Lynette asked. "Who?'

"The bartender!" Holly said, exasperated already. "Sean kind of knows him. He noticed you."

"What does that mean?"

"Do you even know who I'm talking about?"

Lynette thought for a minute. "The bartender," she repeated, as though it were coming to her. "Dark-haired guy?" It was a lucky guess.

So she ended up back there with them, the second Friday in a row, and she pretended to recognize the dark-haired guy when he put an oily-looking pink drink in front of her and winked. She let the drink get watery before sipping it. It tasted like a Shirley Temple with vodka. From down the bar Holly and Sean smirked at her and raised their eyebrows, and Lynette wished for an attack of appendicitis.

She was attractive! Okay, fine! It just wasn't the most interesting thing in the world to her, but Holly acted as though Lynette were wasting something important.

Holly and Sean weren't her friends, exactly, but they took Lynette's reticence, her focus on her work, her indifference to her looks as a challenge. This bartender veered toward chubby, but Lynette was awkward, so they probably figured each had an approximately equal deficit. There was an undercurrent of making fun, and Lynette didn't know how to show them that she recognized it. Who knew whether the chubby bartender did.

There were some superficial similarities. She and the bartender were both past forty and both orphans if you didn't count his father, a late-in-life transplant from the Deep South to the Pacific Northwest who hadn't been around for Brent's childhood—Brent, that was her ex-husband's name—but showed up in his son's twenties. And though Brent would make vague claims to sexual experience that sounded not just exaggerated but made up, Lynette was close enough to virginal not to question them.

They were an exact match! Said Holly and Sean.

Holly and Sean broke up and quit, one after the other. Lynette and Brent stayed together.

* * *

Sometimes termites swarmed indoors. It could happen in the tenants' living room, piles of bodies and cast-off wings, dead bugs drifted like sand. This was the season. The termites would appear like a spray of mud where the baseboard met the floor, sudden black flecks against the white paint. Quickly they would be tens and hundreds, thousands before they were through, a horde more like one large, writhing body than many small ones.

Lynette had witnessed a swarm only once, outside, a couple of months after her father-in-law left. She had been walking home with a chair someone down the street had set out for the trash, a lightweight but bulky rattan number that allowed her to see, as she lurched home gripping its arms and with the seat resting on her head, something blowing around her front porch. It was leaves or dirt, caught by a low wind. When she reached the house she lowered the chair and knew, without a single *what the hell* moment, that here was *Reticulitermes hesperus*, swarming out of holes they'd made at the base of her porch.

Her employer gave her a discount to treat the house, five percent for loyal service and another five for her bereavement. *Brent*, she reminded herself, the source of her bereavement. He was recently dead and his father had even more recently left, and she was not so stupid as to think the appearance of the termites was a sign, but she liked the symbolism of it and the order in which events had occurred: she was rid of one repulsive man and then the other, and practically the next thing that happened was her very favorite insect (her pet insect! *ha ha*), one she'd spent her life studying, showed up in the yard that was now hers alone.

Her pet insect was one of several she'd spent her life trying to kill, but still. It was like a part of herself came back to her, in this house she'd never wanted anyway.

Swarmers were the reproductives, all frantic for a mate. If they emerged indoors they were trapped. Unable to get into the soil, they would dry out within a few hours. Mitchell and Prashant would come home to thousands of dead and dying insects, their wings separated from their bodies—picture it, such lavish waste. She would love to see it happen, but she would not stay to clean up because she was not supposed to be there. *It is mine for one year,* Mitchell had told her. That was what a lease was for—of course she knew it: to keep her out.

But she would stay and watch. She would even risk discovery to see the insects pouring from the baseboard, so many it seemed the wall should burst; there would be her portal. They would stream toward the front window, and cover the glass so it vibrated and the light in the room dimmed and dappled. Then the first few would drop to the floor, having lost their wings. More would come after them, and for several minutes there would be a rush from baseboard to window to floor, a black gust.

She would watch until the stream slowed, and the termites were mostly down, a mass of bodies on bodies, desiccating and thwarted. They would be slower moving now but inches thick, and she would slip out the front door while they still twitched and suffered. What would it be like to die by drying?

She would cross back to her side to wait. Mitchell and Prashant would see the insects as soon as they came in. They would make the horrifying discovery and come to her. They would lodge their hysterical complaints, and tell the hippies.

* * *

Prashant's closet was as unremarkable as Mitchell's. She took a pair of his socks and dropped them in Mitchell's sock crate. She put salted water in one cube of one ice tray. She moved Mitchell's other Bible, the one with the red cover, and slid Prashant's makeshift bookshelves a few inches toward the window. And when the war game reappeared, she moved one tiny plastic man or plane or tank per day, Libya to Japan, Manchuria to Australia, Alaska to Peru.

The hippies were harder to affect. Kicking that first raised bed did nothing but bruise her heel. She poked holes in the bags of soil and peat and manure, and hid a box of screws under the shed. She considered scraping some of the mud off the walls of the furnace room, to transfer termites to the raised beds, but she couldn't do it. She didn't want to. Any damage would be minimal, besides. These were only the workers; they couldn't reproduce.

While the hippies built their raised beds, Lynette let herself in to the other side of the duplex to make her small adjustments. *It is mine, Mrs. Collins. It is mine for one year.* And at night she made adjustments to the yard.

* * *

After a few more days the intermittent drilling stopped for good. She'd noticed the provisional stop, the usual whooshing back in of quiet, and then some time later—twenty minutes, an hour?—she noticed the quiet had persisted. She looked out her kitchen window to survey the backyard. Though she'd been monitoring the hippies' progress, the six raised beds surprised her in their finishedness. They faced north and south in two rows of three. They would surely fade to gray, but for now they were starkly red coming up out of the green-brown of the lawn, foreign and geometric.

They had to be filled, and the vegetables planted and tended (did the hippies expect to use her water?), and these were relatively quiet chores, unlikely to disturb her studious tenants. Maybe Mitchell and Prashant would allow them to come and go now as they pleased.

Catty and Antoine stood at the north end of the yard and admired their work. Lynette watched them, and she saw Catty raise her hand and smile and the tenants come loping across the lawn. Mitchell and Prashant gestured at the raised beds, swung their arms north and south in exclamation over—what? Symmetry, perhaps. Besides the colors, and the finishedness, the beds' symmetry was most striking. The hippies had measured and straightened, and they'd pounded the stout interior posts into the ground.

And now they were giddy with their success. Look at what they had done! An ugly yard in the middle of the city, and they had made it theirs. It was theirs to share with Mitchell and Prashant, and to tame and beautify further. The crabapple would come down, and the shed too, and eventually the house with the termites in it. Lynette would skulk around, invisible, as her property was razed and rebuilt around her.

She went outside, down the stairs and around to the back from the south, on "her" side. She strode to the first bed. The four of them—the hippies and the tenants, the farmers and the Christians—drifted toward her. Lynette looked inside the bed. Just grass so far.

"They look like coffins," she said.

"They'll look different when they're full," Catty answered.

"What's next?"

"We'll fill them and start planting," Antoine said.

All four looked at her, waiting, and she was reminded of the abrupt quiet after the drill stopped.

"How will you water?" she asked.

Antoine again. "We have jugs of water in the truck, for the trees, but it would be helpful if we could use your spigot. We brought our own hose. And if it's okay with you, we thought about installing rain barrels."

"How did you find me?"

Catty slid her eyes to Antoine. "We knew which neighborhoods had large lots," she said.

"You can look up lot dimensions," Mitchell added. "That's public."

Lynette ignored him. "So you picked some and went around, appraising them for your purposes?"

"Yes," Catty said, and Antoine said, "That's when we came to your door."

"You looked in the window."

"I apologize for that," Antoine said. "It was hard to tell if anyone was here."

She glanced at Mitchell and Prashant, who appeared unfazed that their new friend Antoine had come right up on her porch and looked inside her house. The tenants met her eyes, and Mitchell shrugged. She couldn't affect any of them.

The heat started at the base of her neck and slithered up her scalp. "Are you done making noise?" she asked.

Catty tilted her head. "I'm sorry?"

"With the drill. Planting and watering and so forth—that won't bother the tenants."

There was one short bark out of Mitchell, which ended in a smirk, and Catty corrected her. "Mitchell and Prashant," she said, as though Lynette didn't know their names.

"It won't bother us," Prashant said. "We've already talked about it."

"We need one more day to drill in hardware for bird netting. But after that we'll start coming earlier in the morning," Catty explained. "And we'll be quiet." She smiled at Lynette, to suggest she might have considered her at all.

*   *   *

Lynette had married Brent because he pursued her. She'd stayed because it seemed easier than the upheaval of leaving. Certainly she'd been pursued before, but never with such persistence. What was the big deal for him? She had not been very responsive, which was maybe part of the initial appeal, but how do you say to someone, *Listen, it's not that I am mysterious, it's that your interest does not interest me*?

Certain animals freeze when they think they are being pursued. They play dead. She was one of those animals.

Still, pursuit made you pay some attention, like maybe this person is on to something. Maybe I could be part of a passionate love affair.

It turned out not to be that. It turned out only that her co-worker Sean sort of knew him and thought he seemed lonely, what with his dad—who sounded like a demanding old bastard—sucking up a lot of time and energy. So he could use a little female companionship.

And Sean knew this lady Lynette at work who was quiet and kind of odd but also weirdly hot, not to mention over forty and still single like Brent was, so they'd bring her to the bar some time and he could look her over. Come on, man, why the hell not?

Some of this was reported by her co-worker Holly. Some of it Lynette guessed.

After her genuine, non-strategic indifference failed to deter Brent, she let herself be borne along by his pursuing, about which she did have a preliminary flash of curiosity, and which resulted in a pregnancy and then very quickly a miscarriage, an experience more strange than traumatic but one that made him clamp down on her, when she should have taken the opportunity to extricate herself—shouldn't she? Or maybe it was inevitable that the whole thing would play out the way it did. Anyway, it was long over. What was the point of regret?

They got married, the pregnancy, in a way, still heavy inside them both, with her play-acting at guilt for her aging body's rejection of it. Her relief was huge, it was obscene, and it made her feel expansive and tolerant: not *that*, thank god not that, and so *this*? This she could handle. It was just what people did, right—get married?

Once in a while he stirred something in her, and she would rally to a bit of loyalty, almost. Or to an acknowledgment that she was, if she had to ally herself one way or another, classifiably heterosexual.

Why did marriage have to mean cohabitation and being together all the time, though? The kind of relationship she thought might suit her—sustained and monogamous but periodic—didn't appear to be on offer anywhere, but was she truly the only person who might want to go out or have sex just once a month or so?

God, though, she didn't like when he touched her, not really at all. Early on, she got herself sort of hummingly through it by letting her mind leave the scene. But one time he noticed her actually humming. "What is that? Hold music?" he'd asked, which surprised her for being so clever and apt that she laughed. He rolled off and didn't talk to her for two full days.

The silent treatment was glorious. Lynette thought he seemed calmer, too, after those two days, and this appeared to be their way forward: leave each other alone. It worked for a while, but he got fat and resented her for it, and needed a knee replacement and resented her for it, and she never got pregnant again, so he resented her for that. What used to be almost companionable quiet was filled with his stomping and muttering. Then when she did not immediately assent to his suggestion that they let his dad live with them (they'd been married a few years; she'd already had a belly full of her father-in-law), he swept a dirty casserole dish off the kitchen counter and roared ridiculously when it only bounced on the linoleum. She snickered, and he left the house and came back hours later and told her they were buying a duplex. She didn't respond, which wasn't the silent treatment. There was just nothing to say.

After that it was ten years before he died, years she spent being married the way she spent them doing laundry or mowing the lawn. People said marriage was hard work, but divorce would be a project too, something she considered like she considered rehanging the front door. In each case the fix would be gratifying but the process a trial, and there were work-arounds: pull up on the handle to open in the one case; work late, sleep in the guest room, hum very quietly in the other.

But when he died her beautiful, ardent relief was even more obscene than it had been the first time.

* * *

When Lynette heard knocking that evening, she was surprised to look out and see Prashant on the front porch, alone.

She opened the door. "Hello," she said. "Come in."

"Thank you," he said, stepping inside and easing the door shut behind him.

"Well? What now? Did Mitchell send you?"

"Mrs. Collins, have you been in our apartment?"

He said it with that incongruous British accent, in a low, kindly voice like an old man. He stooped above her, and though she wasn't Catholic and didn't know what confession was like, she imagined it could be like this: an accusation in a dim entryway from someone tall and shape-shifting—both Indian and British, young and old, gentle and disapproving, God and man.

She made a sound at the back of her throat that was loud inside her head.

"Because some things seem a bit off," he went on. "I think my bookshelves were shoved over a few centimeters. Is that possible?"

"I suppose it is possible." Those bookshelves had been awkward to wield. She hadn't moved them very far.

"If you need to get in, you're supposed to tell us. I believe that's our right."

"Yes." The heat bloomed across the top of her chest and tucked itself in under both arms. "Mitchell asks for a lot."

He made no acknowledgment of that. "I thought I would tell you this now as well—we won't renew our lease this summer. We have other plans for housing next year."

First there was relief, then she asked, "What about the hippies?"

"I'm sorry?"

But he knew who she meant. He inhaled and looked away. "They already planted trees," he said, and looked back at her. "Why would you—" he started.

She waited, but he only shook his head.

"There are termites," she told him. It was a confession, the first time she'd said it out loud. "In the house. I'll need to have it treated."

He stared at her. Seconds accrued, and his expression didn't change. Finally he said, "Perhaps we will look to move out sooner, then." He continued to stare at her. She stared back. "And Mrs. Collins, I think we would be entitled to our deposit money."

It would be a lot for her to come up with at once. Her heart moved up and up, warming her armpits, then her throat until it lodged in her skull, fitting itself around her brain and her sinuses and pulsing there.

"I will consult my father," he went on. "He's a lawyer."

"In India."

"Nevertheless."

She didn't mean to argue with him. "That's fine," she said now to Prashant, priest and demon. "Because I think I might just sell the house anyway."

"Well," he said. "We will let you know our plans."

He left and she went downstairs. The mud tubes were as they'd been, only a means of transport. All the destruction was above her. She'd leaned a mirror to cover the gash in the living room baseboard, but had peeked behind it a hundred times. That gash and this mud were like scabs or pimples or sheets of peeling skin, hideous but fascinating things that she knew she shouldn't touch.

* * *

The next morning Lynette looked out the kitchen window to see the pear trees, adjacent to that old crabapple, which had started to leaf, and the decrepit toolshed that was like a crypt for whatever it still held. The bags of soil and peat and manure were there; the beds like coffins remained.

Surely Prashant had told Mitchell about the termites, surely they would tell the hippies—also about her claiming she would sell the house. Selling had not occurred to her, not seriously, before she mentioned it to Prashant last night. She would have to treat the termites; she would have to do it now. And she would have to disclose both incidents of infestation. But it was amazing what people would buy. She could so easily foist this burden upon some stranger.

Still, the house was hers alone and you had to live someplace. And entropy was the state of the whole spinning world. She could feel her heart now, trapped and furious inside her. This would be their final day of drilling, the hippies had said. When they came she would have one last assurance that the tenants were in class.

Later though, Mitchell would stage a dramatic confrontation. He would make indictments and demands out of Prashant's sober questions. But the hippies would not be afraid of termites—of course they wouldn't; they would see the bugs as benign, masters of decomposition. They knew, or would quickly learn, that these termites would not eat healthy live trees or make the great leap from the house to the raised beds in the yard. Neither would Catty and Antoine be afraid of her selling. They had improved her land already, and lots of people around here would see their continued presence that way too.

She knew what they all would do. She knew it like prophecy. Here she waited, because of things she herself had said. She waited for them, and she waited to see what she would do with her own property and all that it contained. It was entirely her decision—and more than anything now, that was what vexed her.

MOTHER AND CHILD

Mother watches him from a stand of poplars growing out of the dunes. She's kept still for five minutes already and the boy hasn't turned around. Mother is wearing dark clothes and will be hard to see among the trees, she knows. She is skinny as a poplar, and the hollows in her face darken with the dusk.

Mother gave him a red plastic shovel and a matching sandcastle mold, and sat behind him. She watched the water and felt it pour into her, moving through her limbs and torso. When the child was engrossed, she eased herself up and backed away from him, listening as his voice grew fainter. Jesus loves me thisIknow, he sang, for the Bible tellsmeso. Little onesto himbe long. They are weakbut he isstrong. He still sings. She can almost hear him.

No one else is around. It's a Monday in October and she can look right and see the empty parking lot several hundred yards away and the pier beyond that, and look left and see nothing but sand for what seems like forever. She could walk along the beach for what would seem like forever. But if she moves he will look up and stop her. Mom! he will say, and she will say, I'm right here, I'm right here. Baby, I'm right here. Baby, she calls him, though he protests. I'm five, he says, not a baby. She won't say it yet, though. She will keep still. She can do that. She can dissolve into these trees and vanish herself.

Child turns. Mom? he says. Mom? He abandons the toys and stands up. He blinks and looks around, waiting in the almost-dark for the boundaries between earth and water and sky to emerge.

Mother inhales and goes rigid while he looks up and down the sand for her. For a moment she considers backing up farther into the trees and climbing the tallest dune, away from him. But she doesn't because the sweetest part is coming. Mom! Mom! He runs now, in wide loops, getting nowhere, and then he stops and crumples to the sand. Mama! The old terror. Child knows he has to cry because crying is what makes her come back, but every time he's afraid she won't.

Mother counts to sixty, then steps out from the trees and the water evaporates from her body. She wonders how she looks, unvanishing herself like this, if it seems a part of nature itself is coming forward. She calls to him, and here, here: here is the purest instant. It's only a flash, when he looks up and sees her smiling with her arms out and knows he is saved. He runs at her and she picks him up, soothing—Shh, shh, baby, I'm here, I'm here—and already the instant is past.

Where were you? he accuses. He wants to kiss her and hit her and yank her head around by its ponytail. He doesn't move while she strokes his hair. I was only looking at the trees, she tells him. They're turning color, see? I was here all along, baby. I was just looking at the trees.

* * *

Child lies in bed, at night or during his nap, and thinks about hurting babies. It makes his teeth feel funny, so sometimes he gets up and eats handfuls of coffee, right from the big can, but only when his mother is away. He scoops his fingers in and bites and crunches, not with his back teeth, like normal eating, but with the fronts. He pretends he is a beaver. He pretends he is a beaver eating a baby's head that tastes like coffee. He's heard babies have soft heads, and he wonders what that means, if they're soft like a ripe nectarine or soft like a kitten or soft like other things that are soft. Sometimes it's not his teeth that feel funny, but his throat or his chest, like something's there, touching him. Maybe it's a baby. He wants to hold the baby that might be touching him. He would be careful. He wouldn't hurt it, not really, but he would hold it by one arm and swing it, lightly while he sang. Je sus lovesthe little chil dren, allthe children oftheworld. Then he would swing it rougher. It would be hard not to, even though his teeth would feel like they were floating in his head. He would swing it in a circle and let go. He wouldn't be able to help it; the baby would slip. Down would come baby. Down, but first up.

He pushes in the babies' eyes and yanks on arms and legs so they'll hang loose. He steps on fat squishy tummies and bends back fingers and stretches mouths from their corners until they rip. He bites to bleeding where he can, noses and toes and ears, and he twists necks around as far as they'll go. He pulls out hair and sits on rib cages and presses his thumb into throats.

Afterward, the babies lie around his room, crying, and this is when he wants the coffee. If he can't have it he chews on the corner of his sheet instead, or his own wrist, like a trapped animal, a feral boy all bony and matted. He prefers the coffee's crunchiness, though, and the way it makes him feel—fast and tingly and relieved. Coffee is for grown-ups, but it's not hard for him to get. He climbs up on the counter and stands to reach the high shelf. It's easy.

After the coffee he does his prayers, even if it's just for a nap. NowI layme, rockabye baby, downto sleep my soulto keep, ifI should die before I wake, my soulto take whenthe bough breaks.

* * *

Mother lets him help her cook. They chop vegetables for a big pot of soup, celery and carrots and tomatoes and peppers and onions. She gives him the wooden pig cutting board, some stalks of celery, and a serrated knife as long as his forearm. With a matching knife she dices a pepper while he watches. Don't put your fingers in the way of the knife, she says, sliding the blade ever so lightly across the tops of her knuckles. Touch only the handle, she says, as she runs the pad of her forefinger along the blade. Don't do this, she says, and holds a strip of pepper over the pot on the stove while she brings the knife toward herself, stopping when the blade reaches her thumb and a small piece of pepper falls into the pot. Okay, she says, and points at the wooden pig with her knife. Go ahead.

Child takes his own knife and very slowly cuts the brown shriveled tip off a stalk of celery. She watches him pick up the tip, place it in the palm of his other hand, and lick it off and chew. Then he chops off another tiny piece, and another, leaving them on the pig, and Mother moves her cutting board and her pepper to the kitchen table behind the counter, where she can see him but he can't see her. Remember, she says, be careful. Don't touch the knife to your hand. Don't ever handle the blade. He nods.

They chop. Child likes how the celery feels under his knife, the way it resists and then yields, and he likes the snapping sound it makes when he cuts through.

Mother gets up and scrapes her pepper into the pot, selects another pepper and two onions, and sets them on the table. Then she scoops the handful of celery bits the boy has produced into her palm and drops those in the pot too. Child peers in after his celery. He liked the pile he was making and is sad to see it go.

Mother isn't careful but she's fast, and she manages not to cut herself even while keeping one eye on her child. She has to watch. She doesn't want him to hurt himself. When he stops his slow cutting and studies the knife she lowers her head, but she can see him turn around to look at her. Oh, I forgot something, she says, and gets up. She heads toward the bathroom but stops just outside the kitchen. Mom? she hears him ask. Mother counts thirty seconds and peeks around the corner. She can see him only from the back, but it's clear he's still holding the knife and that his other hand is raised to chest level. He looks around once more, and she ducks back into the hallway. She can feel her pulse all over her body.

Child wants to do it. He's scared, but he's going to do it. He wants to know if skin is like celery, if it resists and yields and snaps, if it feels good to cut it up and make a pile. He positions the tip beneath his pointer finger and pulls down diagonally. It doesn't hurt.

Mother steps back into the kitchen. He hears her and wheels around, his palm out with a gash bleeding into his sleeve. He wants to show her he isn't crying, and for the smallest moment she thinks he means the lesion as an offering. For an even smaller moment her stomach turns, but then he does cry and she rushes to him. It hurts now, and he shouts at her: You did it! She takes his hand and pulls him to the sink. You did it! When the water hits his wound he tries to pull away, but she holds him. It's okay, it's okay, baby, she says, shh, it's okay.

A clean towel is lying on the counter and she presses it to his palm and wraps it around his hand. She picks him up and he clings to her, sobbing. You did it! You did it!

❊ ❊ ❊

Every Sunday Mother goes to church. She wears her blue dress or her beige one and sits in the back. She stands up with the people and sits down with them and holds the hymnal while they sing, and even shakes hands when the preacher says it's time. Good morning, she says. Peace of Christ, she says. But while the people have their service, Mother listens only to God.

God makes noises and Mother translates. Sometimes he tells her about colors or sounds. Green and yellow, God says. Black and red. Birdsong and lawn mowers and dripping water. Car horns. And sometimes he gives her reminders: hair teeth feet, underpants shirt shoes, refrigerator pillow front door.

The people smile at the strange skinny woman who sits in the back, but they've mostly stopped asking her to Bible studies and potlucks.

She always says no, and sometimes she doesn't answer at all, just smiles back and shakes her head, as though she doesn't know their language. At first they thought she was some kind of refugee, with her shadowed eyes and teeth and that wolf baby, her son, who makes their children uneasy.

This morning Mother is wearing her beige dress. The preacher is praying, and Mother prays too. Dear God, she says, dear God dear God dear God dear God. God waits a minute and Mother waits too and then God says something and it means: take the money.

When the collection basket gets to her, Mother puts in her five dollars. She spots a twenty and touches it. She pretends to fold the twenty into her palm and passes the basket to the next person, who believes he has just seen the woman wrestle with Satan and win. He is proud of her but still, after the service he will warn the preacher.

Mother sits with her fist in her lap, but God stops talking. He knows she didn't take it. She wants to cry, but no one cries in church, so she bites the insides of her cheeks to stop the tears.

After church she goes into the hall and drinks coffee because everyone has to. A man stands next to Mother and drinks his coffee and says, Good morning, how are you? He is being Christian; there but for the grace of God go I, he thinks. Mother means to say Good morning, how are you? but she's still upset and so she says Peace of Christ instead. The man laughs and pats her on the shoulder and Mother knows she's turning red inside her beige dress. I mean, she says, and the man pats her again and shouts across the hall to another man and leaves her to empty her foam cup alone.

The coffee is very hot and it takes her a long time to finish. When she finally does she can go get her boy from the nursery. She hopes he'll still be there. She hopes God hasn't already taken him.

❄ ❄ ❄

Child is the only big kid in the nursery today. He tells his mother he hates that, but secretly he's glad. He likes to be the tallest and the oldest, and he likes to be left alone by the teacher ladies, who will be too busy with the babies and toddlers to bother him.

Child sets himself up in a corner with the tub of painted blocks. For most of the hour he builds towers and looks out for encroachments from three toddlers who chase each other in circles. Child puts a leg out as a barrier, and the children tighten their orbit. Sometimes when their parents drop them off and he's there, they don't want to be left. He's a big kid, they know, but they don't want to grow up and be big like him.

Besides the toddlers, there are two babies asleep in the cribs against the far wall, and the teacher lady holds two other babies. Child doesn't know the word ratio, but he understands the concept: the lady is outnumbered. There should be another lady here.

Two of the toddlers miscalculate a turn and smack heads. They scream, and the third toddler screams, and then some of the babies wake up and scream. The teacher lady puts the babies she's holding in two empty cribs and tries to comfort the crying toddlers. The lady looks to Child as though she will start crying too, so he gets up and walks to the cribs, which are stacked like tiny bunk beds. He reaches with his good hand—the one without the bandage, the one that didn't get cut when he was making soup—into one of the bottom bunks and caresses the baby inside on the arm. He tickles her hand and she grasps his finger, but doesn't stop crying. He jiggles the finger a little inside her grip. Hey, hey, he says. It's all right. Don't cry. Baby, don't cry. Shh, it's all right. There's one baby who's stayed quiet. Sitting up in his crib, the quiet baby stares at Child.

Rockabye baby inthe treetop, he sings to the little girl holding his finger. Whenthe wind blowsthe cradlewill rock. He extricates the finger and pats her on the tummy, gently, in time with his singing. Anddown willcome baby, cradleandall.

Child looks over his shoulder, and the lady is still fussing with the toddlers, so he moves his hand to the baby's head. He strokes her on the temple and tells her it's all right. He rests his palm on her forehead and spreads his fingers. Her head doesn't feel soft to him. It feels like his own head, only smaller. He presses his fingertips against her skull, lightly, and then harder, and then as hard as he can. Child knows the quiet baby can see him do this through the bars between the cribs, but it's all right because babies can't talk. Child grits his teeth and keeps pressing, but he can't do it very long because his arm gets tired. He lets go. The girl baby is still crying, but not any louder than before.

When the lady gets the toddlers calmed down, she comes over to relieve Child. Oh *thank* you, she says. That's so *help*ful of you to check on the babies. She's only a college student, an early-education major, and this kid has made her so uncomfortable she wonders if she should switch to business. He slips past her and goes back to sit in the corner, where he waits to see if he'll want to eat coffee.

After church his mother comes to get him, and the words are there: I squeezed a baby's head, but he doesn't say them.

⁕ ⁕ ⁕

Mother takes her child to the mall to buy new shoes. Mother loves the mall. It is cool and bright and full of glass. It makes her feel calm and very very clean. Pretty salesgirls smile and ask if they can help, and she always says yes, yes they can. Where might I find curtains, she asks, or lingerie, or jeans size two, or menswear, or children's shoes? This whole trip to the mall she doesn't ask for anything she's really looking for except the children's shoes, and she already knows where those are. But she likes to make the pretty girls happy, so she lets them lead her around stores to browse new, sweet-smelling, well-organized items she doesn't need.

They've already bought the shoes. Can we please go home? her boy asks. We've been here all day. We have not, she answers, but we'll look at just one more big store and then we can go. Inside the store she asks a handsome boy for the jewelry counter, and he walks her over to costume jewelry and says his name is Kris and that he'd be happy to help if she needs further assistance.

Jewelry is near handbags, and while Mother looks at earrings and watches, Child wanders to a display of bags shaped like animals, Scottie dogs and cats and even birds. Mother keeps one eye on him, and Kris keeps an eye on them both. She's kind of cute, he thinks, but awfully skinny. She doesn't look old enough, but the skinny kid must be hers.

Honey, don't go too far, Mother calls, but not loudly. Child doesn't nod or say okay. She watches him play with the animals for a minute, then backs up a few feet to fondle long beaded necklaces hanging on a circular rack. The beads are translucent and smooth, like colored bits of ice, and she presses a handful to her forehead. Kris watches her and wonders if this is a shoplifting operation—she leaves the kid alone as a distraction so no one will pay attention to her.

Behind the necklaces are brooches, which don't interest Mother, and then a rack of hats, with veils and feathers and wide floppy brims. Church hats. She tries on a pink woven one with a thick black ribbon and a veil of dotted tulle, which she pulls down and tucks under her chin. She can see her boy through the veil, but she vanishes a little behind it. Mother lifts the hat off her head and puts it back. Behind the hats are umbrellas and scarves and light gloves for fall, and behind those is a huge makeup counter. Kris follows her as she walks slowly to the makeup, but before the pretty smiling girl in a white lab coat can ask if she needs help, Mother zips around the other side of the counter and the boy is lost to her and she is lost to Kris.

Mother vanishes. She is fast now, and pleasantly breathless. She passes rack after rack of skirts and blouses and jackets, then moves into the juniors' section, where everything sparkles. She speeds through girls' and boys' and men's and stops in housewares to finger an ironstone bowl and ask an old woman whose nametag says Frann about wineglasses.

In housewares Mother feels safe. She is in her grandmother's beautiful home. She is just a girl, and she can take a nap when she wants, on a bed whose quilt and sheets and pillows all match, and she can sit at a dining table set with crystal and china in Grandma Frann's patterns. She can stay here until she hears her name over the loudspeaker, when she will rush off to wherever she is summoned. For now, though, she can relax because everyone is safe.

Mother sits on a sofa and turns on the lamp behind it to inspect the upholstery. It is a soft textured green, so lovely she could cry, and the lamp's base is all soldered vines and rosebuds. Oh, she breathes, running her hand over the sofa's back and arm. Oh, she says again, trailing her fingertips down the lamp's metal greenery.

Her grandmother approaches the sofa, smiling, and Mother smiles back. The old woman leans over and says in a low voice, Ma'am, they found your son. Oh, Mother says. Oh, oh yes. She jumps up and looks around. But he was right here! I thought he was right here. Oh my heavens! Yes, well, Frann says, come with me. Mother tries to get excited about seeing her boy. She tries to anticipate his relief at seeing her, but there was supposed to be a loudspeaker.

Mother follows Frann into a hidden room behind menswear, and there is her child, sitting in an office chair and holding a Scottie bag with his bandaged hand, and two of Kris's fingers with his good one. Her boy wails when he sees her. Mama! Oh honey, she says, and picks him up. It's okay, it's okay, I'm here. I thought you were right behind me! She holds him and rubs his back, then she tries to set him down but he won't let go.

There's another man in the room. Mother turns to him. He's very handsome. Thank you, she says. I thought he was right behind me. Yes, the man says. Right. That happens. The man and Kris and Frann all wonder if they should call someone, the police or child protective services.

Mother feels the Scottie bag pressing against her neck, and she reaches up and pries it out of her boy's hands. She tries to offer it to the man, but Child screams. No! He said I could have it. Oh no, Mother says, shaking her head. No. The man takes it, but holds it away from himself. He doesn't want to touch the bag the kid had pressed to his face. It's okay, the man says. I did say he could have it. No, Mother says. No. It's not ours. Ma'am, just take it. I can't sell it like this. He wants to punish her a little. He knows he's not going to call anyone. He lifts up the bag and she can see it's wet and the leather is stained. We'll just write it off. I'll pay for it then, Mother says. The man sighs. Ma'am, it's a hundred and fifty dollars. Mother works her jaw, and her child screams. He said I could have it! The handsome man and the old woman and the boy Kris stare at her. Finally, she nods at them. Thank you all the same, she says and walks out of the room. No! No! the child cries. It's mine! He said I could have it. It is mine! She walks through the store while he screams at her. It's mine! I hate you! People turn and she ignores them. She marches outside, but then she must go halfway around the mall to find her parking spot. He screams all the way.

When they get to the car he calms down and lets her strap him into his car seat. No you don't, she says. What? he asks. You don't hate me. Child looks out the window. Sometimes he does hate her. Hey, she says, grabbing him by the chin. You don't hate me. You love me. She grips him harder. That dog was mine, he says, and starts to cry again. I loved it. She digs in to his jaw with her thumb and forefinger so his teeth part and his lips open. I love you, he says, and it's true. Okay, good, Mother responds and lets go. I love you too.

They are quiet for the ride home, but when they pull into the driveway Child says, What about my new shoes? and Mother doesn't know where in the mall she left them so she puts her head on the steering wheel and cries.

❊ ❊ ❊

Child hasn't forgotten about the dog bag. His mother told him he would, but he hasn't and it's been two days. The man said he couldn't sell the dog since Child cried on it and got it wet, and that probably meant it was thrown away. This makes Child so sad he can't stand it. He didn't care about the wet spot.

He knows the dog isn't real, but he can't help thinking about *The Velveteen Rabbit*, a book he had to hide it made him so sad. He still won't let himself remember where he put that book. If his mother had let him keep the dog bag he would never have thrown it away like the velveteen rabbit got thrown away. He would have kept it forever and put only his best toys in it, and he would have given it to his own boy some day.

This afternoon he pleaded with his mother again to go back to the store and get the dog bag but she said, We're done talking about the dog bag. I don't want to hear another word about it, do you understand me? A little part of Mother regrets not letting him keep it.

Child doesn't know why she asks if he understands. She always asks that. But all he said was, It's not fair! and ran outside to the swing that hangs from the tree in the front yard, where he's been sitting by himself for a long time now. I loved that dog, he whispers, while he twists and untwists the swing's chains. I loved him.

A few of their neighbors have noticed him all alone in that yard that's not really a yard, just a strip of weeds with a half-dead tree and a swing too close to the road. They noticed and when it got dark enough they closed their blinds.

What makes Child saddest about *The Velveteen Rabbit* is not that the rabbit got thrown away but that the boy never found out his old toy turned into a real rabbit and lived happily ever after. This causes Child such anguish that he puts his head on his knee and cries, right there in the front yard. If he knew that the man at the store took the dog home for his own kids or cleaned it up and put it back out to be sold, he would feel okay. But he'll never know.

Child's palm itches and he sits up and picks at the tape holding the bandage to his hand. He peers in, but it smells bad and he can't see, so he pulls the bandage off, even though his mother told him to leave it alone. In a line across his palm is a series of small scabs. He scratches one and it doesn't bleed so he scratches another. That one bleeds a little, but the one after that doesn't bleed at all. He plays a guessing game. If a scab bleeds, that means the dog got thrown away; if it doesn't, it didn't.

The last scab Child scratches doesn't bleed, but it hardly matters. A line of red is trickling down his arm. Child moans and stamps his feet. It was mine! he yells and jumps off the swing to whip its chains against the tree. He wipes his bloody hand over his face and hair and flings himself to the ground and kicks his legs in the rhythm of his speech. It was mine! Kick, kick, kick.

Child is out of breath and getting cold. He rolls over and picks up the bandage, then changes his mind and drops it. He stands up and purposely does not brush himself off, and on his way inside he imagines his blood making a trail. In the entryway he stands on the linoleum and calls to his mother and as she comes down the hall with a pile of laundry he holds his dripping hand over the beige carpet, the one he's not supposed to walk on with shoes.

She dumps the laundry on a chair except for a white T-shirt, which she ties around his hand. Oh honey, what did you do! Why didn't you leave that alone? she says, and leads him into the bathroom. She notices the blood on the floor but doesn't mention it. She'll take care of him, then scrub the carpet after he goes to bed.

In the bathroom Mother washes his hand in the sink, and he flinches when the soap gets into the cut. Oh my baby, she keeps saying, my sweet baby, what happened? She wraps a washcloth around his hand, and then she draws a bath and undresses him and makes him get in.

She cleans him with another washcloth and kisses him and sings to him and calls him honey and baby, but he is silent because she doesn't say anything about the dog bag. When she turns from the tub to look in the cupboard for a new bottle of shampoo, he whispers, I hate you. He knows she hears him because he can see her face in the mirror.

Mother comes back to the tub and lathers his hair and finishes his bath, and he is still her honey and her baby. She dries him off and puts ointment on his wound and attaches another bandage.

Later, in bed, it occurs to Child that if the dog bag were lying in a wastebasket, the person who cleans the store at night might find it and take it home. This makes him feel better, but even so, he might hate his mother. He also might love her. It's hard to tell.

* * *

On the way to church, Mother slams on the brakes at the end of their street. From the back seat her child giggles. Do it again, he says. I thought I saw a squirrel, she tells him, and turns right.

A semi is in the opposing lane. It would be so easy to jerk the wheel to the left. It would be as easy as stomping on the brake pedal. She won't do it of course, but as the truck passes she swerves, just slightly, toward it. She glances in the rearview mirror, but the boy is looking out the window.

Mother takes a shortcut through a construction zone, dormant on the weekend. There are orange cones along the shoulder and between the lanes, and the speed limit is 45. She accelerates to 45, slows back down to 40, then speeds up and up and up again, to 70. The child laughs and claps his hands. Faster! he shouts. Mother presses the gas pedal until the speedometer reads 75, then she takes a curve without braking. Her stomach flips and she wants to move her foot to the brake pedal, but she doesn't do it.

In the mirror she sees the boy has covered his eyes, but he's still giggling. The road straightens out, and way up ahead there's a stoplight. It's red, with one waiting car. Mother lets her car slow, just a little. As they near the stopped car, she accelerates again.

Mother doesn't watch the speedometer anymore, and the stopped car gets closer and closer. Okay, okay, the boy says. Stop now. Stop! And she does, with one tremendous slam that sends her car skidding. She turns the wheel and misses the stopped car, but they go sliding through the red light and come to a halt in the intersection.

The child screams and Mother proceeds to church, obeying all traffic laws and good driving practices. With her eyes on the road she reaches back to rub her boy's shin. Oh sweetie, it's okay, it's okay. He stops screaming, and whimpers now. We're just fine, she says. No one's hurt. But driving too fast isn't funny is it? It's dangerous. She rubs his shin all the way to church.

When she drops him off in the nursery, he needs twelve kisses before he'll let her go, and then Mother heads to the sanctuary feeling serene and ready to listen. She sits in her regular spot and apologizes to God for not taking the money last time. She knows that was a test and she failed. God makes a sound. He forgives her, and Mother is relieved, but he wonders what she will offer him.

Mother thinks for a while and God is quiet and then she knows: her own son. Her only son. She would give him, if God asked.

❊ ❊ ❊

Child knows he should be asleep. He went to bed a long time ago, but he's thinking about Sunday school. This morning the Sunday school teacher asked, What's Hell? The question bored Child. They talked about Hell all the time at church. He stared at the ceiling while the other children answered, It's where bad people go. What are bad people? asked the teacher. People who do bad things, like kill and stuff. Wrong, thought Child. Wrong, said the teacher. People who go to Hell are the ones who don't believe in Jesus. If people do bad things and repent and ask Jesus to come into their hearts, they will go to Heaven.

Child already knew this. Because he believes in Jesus, God forgives his thoughts. When he thinks he hates his mother, or when he thinks about hurting babies, he just says sorry to God. You can say sorry and do anything and it doesn't matter.

Let's pray and really, truly ask Jesus to come into our hearts, the teacher said, and all the children held hands, but Child didn't listen to the prayer because he'd already asked Jesus and Jesus had said yes, which meant Child wouldn't go to Hell for thinking about the babies.

He doesn't think about them every night, only sometimes. Like to-night. There are twenty babies in his room, including the babies from the nursery: the quiet baby, and the one whose head he squeezed, and the others. Child picks up the babies one by one and throws them in the air, then stands back and lets them fall.

When the babies hit the floor their heads crack. Some of the babies are quiet, and some of them cry. Child sits down and looks at what he's done. He sucks his teeth and wishes he had the coffee. He bites on his hand instead, his good hand, and then he bites on his bad one, over the bandage, which tastes salty and sour. Child pulls the bandage off and feels along the ridge of scabs, and he bites again, digging his front teeth into the seam across his palm until it hurts. The flesh resists and yields, and the blood tastes like metal.

Child is tired but relieved. He takes his hand out of his mouth and holds it against his chest. He considers doing his prayers but decides just to say sorry to God later. For not praying and for taking the ban-dage off again and for hurting all those babies.

❊ ❊ ❊

The child follows Mother everywhere. He is unrelenting. She can't even sit in her dark closet alone or in the bathroom with the door locked because he finds her. She can hear his loud breathing outside the door, like a fat old man or a dragon. He wheezes, and she wants to tell him to blow his nose, but she can't speak to him. If she does, it will be harder to vanish herself.

And she's not sure she should vanish. She listens to God, but God's voice is angry and guttural and loud, and she can barely understand him. Vanish, God says. Don't vanish. Vanish. Don't. What? she asks. What? But the boy is so insistent she can't concentrate. After he's driven her to tears with the wheezing, he'll knock on the door. Mom? he asks. She never answers. The knocks come from down low, so she knows he's sitting or even lying down. Mama? Knock knock. Mama, I'm hungry, Mama, I'm scared, Mama, it's cold. Knock knock knock knock knock. Mama Mama Mama.

Child needs a bath and some dinner. His dirty hair hangs in his eyes, and he holds it back with his good hand. Sometimes he pokes at his wound, stirring pus and blood together to make a sticky pink paste, and there's hair in the wound and pus and blood in his hair. He wants his mother to come out, but when she does she scares him with her crying. He doesn't know what's happening to her in the bathroom and the closet.

Mother cries on the closet floor or on the edge of the tub. God shouts at her, and the boy wants things from her, and meanwhile she's melting. She takes off her clothes and her body looks the same, but under the skin is all liquid. If she sways back and forth she hears the sea, but she's too small to hold it. She'll burst and the world will drown. That's why she's vanishing herself. If she vanishes, the sea will vanish with her and her boy will be safe. But she doesn't know if God wants him safe. She can't defy God. Not again.

The boy, her baby, pretends he can't hear the sea inside her. Sometimes in answer to his pleading she stands up and sways for him, from the closet or the bathroom, but he ignores the danger and she cries even harder. She doesn't want to, but she's going to drown him.

❄ ❄ ❄

Child stands in the water, just barely. The waves come up and move around the soles of his shoes, but he steps back before they can get the tops wet. When the waves recede he moves closer to the water. Back and forth he goes. His mother sits behind him on a piece of driftwood. Careful! she calls when the waves touch his shoes or almost do.

Child dodges waves, then he looks for sea glass and interesting rocks, and then he uses his good hand to dig a hole in the wet sand. His bad hand has another new bandage, and he holds his forearm against his chest. His mother sits on her log and shouts Careful! and Watch out!

For a while the waves collapse the front of his shallow hole, but he learns to dig when they recede so that soon he's in up to the elbow. He's pushed his sleeve up as far as it will go, and his arm is numb from working in the cold water. He concentrates on widening the sides, and then he measures the opening: it's one and a half times as wide as his shoe is long.

His mother has stopped telling him to be careful, and he turns to make sure she's there. She is, staring out beyond him. She feels herself slowly filling back up with the sea as she listens and waits for God. Child follows her gaze and watches the orange sun slip into the water and go out.

He goes back to his widening, and the sky darkens and his hole darkens and the water inside it looks black. He measures again: it's two shoe lengths wide now.

He's studying his hole, crouched above it with his nose six inches from the water, when he hears his mother come up behind him. She puts her hand on his head, and he raises his eyes to the horizon all streaked and purple. Isn't it beautiful? she says.

WITH YOU OR WITHOUT YOU

Morley stood in the field, which wasn't a field actually, not at all, but he liked the word "field," liked the expansiveness of it, the way it suggested a sort of infinitude, and what difference did it make to anyone what he called it? None, so that was the word he said to himself: field.

Really, he stood in the yard, facing the line of oaks that marked his property from the neighbors'. His wife and daughter were inside, waiting for him. His wife would ask what he'd been doing standing around in the yard; his daughter would order him to hold still, then pick at his clothes and tell him to hang on while she ran to get her tape measure and her straight pins.

But there was no salvation in staying in the field forever, or walking through the trees to the neighbors'. His stasis was an illusion. He knew this. He wasn't stupid. Last night he'd said so to his wife. "I'm not stupid."

"I know," she'd responded. "I'm not saying you are."

"Jesus, I would never use the word 'colored,' I would never say 'faggot.'"

"Morley, I know."

He'd called the neighbors' daughter "retarded"—because she was; the term wasn't derogatory, it was descriptive—and his wife told him not to say "retarded" because it was like saying "colored" or "faggot."

He'd watched his wife pee and pick at her toenails as she said it, her foot up on the magazine rack and her nightgown hiked above her waist to expose her vein-mottled white thigh, the pressure of her rear end on the toilet seat emphasizing the cellulite. She didn't look at him while she peed and picked—she was pretty limber for a woman in her sixties—and called him a bigot, and he thought, *Well, this is marriage*.

This is marriage, once again. Because she was his second wife.

He'd been working up to tell her he used to wonder if his own daughter might be retarded—he'd never said that before, not to this wife—but instead he just left the room. Later, in bed, when he was quiet and teary and blinking in the dark, she'd rolled over and put her arm around him and whispered, "Morley, I love you." He'd blinked some more. Then she'd kissed him on the ear. "Just don't say 'retarded.'"

It wasn't too much to ask. And it wasn't too much to ask that he come back in to help them after mowing the lawn. This was a nice yard, besides. It would be lovely for his daughter's party. Who'd want a graduation party in a field anyway? Morley dragged the mower around the side of the house and into the garage.

Inside, his wife was cleaning strawberries. "The lawn looks nice," she said.

"Thanks."

"She wants those citronella stakes set out."

"It's barely May." It was May 6. "Are there even any bugs yet?"

"I think we're going for a tiki-lounge mood. And there's that extra set of lawn chairs. The plastic ones. Will you give them a once-over with a rag and put them outside?"

He didn't answer, and she turned around. "Morley? We've got a lot to do still."

"Okay." He would set out the citronella candles and the plastic chairs, and he'd be helpful and congenial and tell his daughter congratulations.

On his way to the bathroom, he ran into her.

"Dad!" She threw open the door of the guest room and accosted him in the hallway.

"Ahh! What?"

She put her hands on her hips and gave him her appraising eye.

"Oh no," he said. "These are work clothes. I was mowing the lawn, and I'm going back out."

But she pinched his sleeve and pulled the seam up to his shoulder. "Shoulder seams go on your shoulders."

"I know."

"This shirt doesn't fit." She let go of the seam.

"It's a work shirt."

"All your shirts are like this." She sighed.

He sighed back. "Congratulations."

"Promise me tonight you'll wear what I laid out for you."

"You laid out my clothes?" Jesus, was he really so bad?

"They're on your bed."

"All right," he said. "All right." He'd resolved to be congenial. "So where do you want those citronellas? I was going to put them in the field for you."

"What?"

"I mean the yard. The yard."

"Oh, anywhere. Around the back, by the trees."

He nodded and walked past her to the bathroom.

Alone again, Morley peed and then stood a minute longer, thinking how it used to be easier to keep the workings of his mind secret, easier to maintain sole hold on his body—and what clothed it. He had tried telling her he actually liked his sleeve seams halfway to his elbows. He liked the baggy crotch, the draggy seat of his pants, but she didn't hear him.

Morley shook off the last drops and zipped his fly and flushed. He switched on the light and looked at himself. Dark hair turned gray, receding some; trifocals; spindly arms; a paunch he could almost hide if he stood up straight; and down below the mirror, hidden in pants too big for him, pale, skinny legs, the hair gone sparse, the calves and ankles sharply tapered and fragile-looking. He was nearly seventy. Maybe big men aged better.

Scrappy, sinewy, taut. Those were the words to describe small men when they were young, and he had been those things, but now he was spindly, skinny, fragile-looking.

There was a time when Rita, his first wife, the mother of his only offspring, had run her hands over his bare shoulders and down his arms, pausing at his biceps to let him flex a little for her. God, he remembered it so clearly.

They were nineteen the first time they had sex. After months of torment, she'd finally let him, the only clues this would be the night a wide grin, a nervous giggle, and her tongue in the hollow of his throat, a place she'd never before put her tongue. Then she took off her underpants and straddled him, and he forced back a sob of relief and gratitude, there behind her parents' barn, long after dark on May 6, 1967.

Now Rita was six years dead and the thought of her was like a thumb pressed into his throat. And he was remarried and his daughter's graduation party had been scheduled for May 6.

He'd tried to avoid it. What about the thirteenth, or the twentieth? But the thirteenth was his new wife's mother's birthday, and on the twentieth they had plans with the Neumans. Any later than that you were too far from the actual graduation in April, and any earlier than the sixth you ran a greater risk of uncooperative weather. Fridays and Sundays were out because, well, people expected parties like this to be on Saturdays, and Morley, what was the problem with the sixth anyway?

Not that he hadn't had previous May 6s cluttered with things to do, and not that he'd planned some secret commemoration—what did he want, to sit by himself and cry all day?—but today was the fiftieth anniversary, taken up by a community college graduation party.

Morley washed his hands. He dried them on his too-big pants and opened the door, half expecting his daughter to ambush him again. He needed to get the citronellas and the plastic chairs out of the garage, but first he wanted to see what he was supposed to wear tonight.

At the foot of the bed were a pair of pants and a shirt he'd put in the Goodwill bag months ago. Since his daughter's graduation she'd been living in his house, so he'd pulled out the clothes meant for charity and let her alter those. These khakis on his bed she'd hemmed two inches but said there wasn't a lot she could do about the inseam without major reconstruction, which probably wasn't worth it for a pair of Dockers.

Still, she'd measured his inseam for future reference, tapping him in the crotch with her tape measure as she did it. He'd jumped and said "Jesus!" and later he'd asked his wife what a person could do with an associate's degree in fashion design.

"She could work at a tailor shop. Or a department store, in alterations."

Fantastic. His daughter was headed for a life of tapping men's crotches at Macy's.

Sometimes he wished she really were retarded. If she fit some diagnosis, he could point to that. Look, he could say, Down's syndrome (like the little girl who lived behind them, the one he'd called retarded last night in front of his wife). But his daughter was just a bit odd, with an IQ only slightly below average and perhaps a touch of Asperger's, though as her long-ago pediatrician had pointed out, people with Asperger's often had very high IQs.

"She's herself," Rita used to say. "There's nothing wrong with her, Morley. She's stepping to her own beat."

And his current wife seemed to have the same attitude, willing to let his daughter follow her whims, to celebrate her small successes, to have this overgrown girl live with them periodically. Morley knew he should be grateful, but he suspected his wife indulged herself. Her own two children were bona fide grown-ups who lived far away.

Of course, his daughter was a bona fide grown-up too. Or she should be, at thirty. God, she was *thirty*. People were often astonished to learn how old she was, but it wasn't a case of one's looking good for one's age. Her clothes fit, sure, but their plainness made Morley think of the Legos she'd had as a kid, those solid Crayola colors and the rectangles of her interchangeable shirts and pants. Plus, her dark hair was cut bluntly to her shoulders and above her eyebrows, she wore no makeup, and she'd had the same round glasses since high school.

Morley picked the newly hemmed Goodwill pants up off the bed. He held them to his waist and stuck one foot out. The pant leg ended just past his ankle, and underneath, the pants he was wearing bagged around his heel. He faced away from the mirror and changed his clothes, and when he looked again he thought: Bony. Gaunt. Spindly, skinny, fragile-looking. *Old.*

He kicked his foot a few inches off the floor, and the pants flapped around his ankle. He tugged the shirt sleeves down, but they ended six inches above his elbows, exposing his withered triceps. He turned one arm over and examined its biceps, pale and nearly hairless, vulnerable, like a baby's head or a woman's bare breast. And this was what he had to look forward to later, this vulnerability, these too-small clothes. This community college graduation party on his private anniversary.

* * *

At the party were the usual supporters, neighbors and family friends and his wife's mother, plus a small gaggle of what Morley referred to as "mall girls." "Who are these mall girls?" he asked his wife when they showed up on the front porch, three of them, with hip bones jutting above waistbands and dark roots peeking out from blond hairdos. The mall girls looked about twenty-two.

"They're her friends. Her classmates. Let them in, Morley."

He did, and they called him Mr. Otis and said thanks for inviting us and followed him through the house to the backyard where the citronella tiki stakes blazed unnecessarily.

"It's really nice, all of this," one of the mall girls said, sweeping her hand to indicate his ersatz field.

"Yeah, what a pretty yard," another one said.

The third one said nothing, and Morley noticed her hair was dark all the way through. Then she turned, and the sun revealed it as auburn.

"Thanks," he answered, and pulled on his shirt sleeve. "Have a soda."

Have a soda. Have a piece of cake. Have a burger. All evening long he pushed food and pulled at his clothes and thought about Rita, bare-assed and nineteen and all he'd ever wanted. He thought about Rita, and tried not to think about Rita, and thought about how no one was named Rita anymore. He watched the mall girls circle his daughter, blunt-haired and aging and clothed in well-fitting rectangles of blue and yellow fabric, and thought about how Rita would have loved it, their daughter stepping to her own beat in the middle of these mall girls, though Rita wouldn't have called them that.

The auburn-haired girl asked him where the bathroom was and he told her and when she came out again she stood next to him and smiled. He smiled back.

"I hear you teach business," she said before he could suggest another soda.

"Accounting," Morley corrected her. "And I'm retired."

"Oh yeah? Where'd you teach at?"

"The university."

"So not where we go."

"Well, no."

She studied him, and he heard her inhale before she introduced herself. "I'm Beatrice."

"You don't say?" It seemed no one was named Beatrice anymore either. He held out his hand, and she took it. They shook. No Ritas, no Beatrices, hardly even any Marys or Susans.

"So what advice would you give someone wanting to start a business?" Beatrice asked.

Morley looked over her shoulder. His gaze seemed to ricochet off the line of trees to land on his neighbor, playing piggyback with his little daughter, the one with Down's syndrome. *Don't say retarded,* he thought, then swung his attention back to Beatrice. "I would advise any entrepreneur to hire a good accountant."

"Ha ha, right."

"Would you like a soda?" Morley tugged on his sleeve.

"Nah. I'm serious, though. In today's business climate, with the economy how it was and all of that, is there one super-important piece of advice you'd give? A few words of wisdom?"

What was this about? What had his daughter told the mall girls? Something spiny hitched up from Morley's gut to seize him under the chin. He felt his nostrils flare.

"I'm not a businessman."

"But Chloe said—"

"I can't imagine what she said. My daughter—"

"Just that you would help us, is all."

"My daughter is a little dense, I'm afraid. As regards her father."

"What does that mean?" Beatrice asked. She lifted one side of her mouth in a sneer, and Morley took a small step back. "Like, so what, she doesn't know all about your job?"

"I need to check on the grill, Beatrice." Morley nodded at her. As he turned away she called after him.

"Hey, Mr. Otis!"

He kept walking, pretending not to hear. *It's Dr. Otis,* he wanted to tell her.

"That was rude," he heard the girl say. "Jeez, what's the big deal?"

Morley's step wavered, but he proceeded to the grill. He picked up the tongs to scrape at some charred bits stuck to the grate, and as he scraped he tugged at his left pant leg with his right shoe, then traded off: right pant leg, left shoe. The spiny thing gave him a shake, and he tried to swallow it down.

My daughter is a little dense. Would Beatrice report what he'd said? Those were some ill-chosen words.

While Morley scraped and tugged, his neighbor galloped over with his little girl. Around in circles they went, her face flashing by every few seconds, its features so conspicuous. What would that be like, to have everyone know at a glance what was wrong with you?

Freeing. It would be freeing, but only if that were the way you'd always been. At this point Morley wouldn't want everyone to know what was wrong with him, partly because what was wrong was unnamable.

For a while, what was wrong with Rita had seemed that way too—though the oncologist had named it plainly. But only toward the end, when the cancer grew beyond its host, when it bloomed from the inside out and pushed through her ribcage, could he believe it. He had actually seen cancer.

You could see Down's syndrome. You could see cancer sometimes. But you couldn't see an IQ just slightly below average and a touch of Asperger's. And you couldn't see grief and malaise and this wearying rage.

"Hi Dad."

Morley jumped, then pretended he hadn't, and resumed his scraping. He worked at the grill for a second before looking up at his daughter. And at Beatrice, who stood behind her. "Hi," he said. He felt his neck get hot.

"Listen," Chloe started, "the girls and I were chatting and we wondered if you'd help us. I know you just talked to Beattie, and maybe she took you off guard." Chloe giggled. "She does that sometimes."

"Who?"

"Beattie. Beatrice."

Beatrice inclined her chin.

Morley scraped vigorously.

Chloe went on. "We have this idea for a business and we want to talk to some professionals to see what they think. Hey, can you stop for a minute?" She put her hand on his wrist.

"Sorry."

She smirked at him and shook her head. Morley set down the tongs. He folded his arms and felt his sleeves ride up. Out of his peripheral vision he spied the other two mall girls—had he been told their names?—crossing the yard toward them.

"So we have this idea," Chloe said. "Will you have coffee with us, and let us ask questions and take notes and brainstorm with you a little?"

"Wait," Morley said. "What are we talking about? What kind of professionals?"

"Business." She shrugged as though it were obvious. "Business professionals."

"I'm an accountant. That's what I tried to tell your friend. Beatrice." He locked eyes with Beatrice, and she smirked too. The other two mall girls lined up next to her and grinned at him.

"But you'd have some thoughts, right?" his daughter asked.

Morley made a small sound of protest way back in his throat. "Come on," he said, "this is a party. Can't we talk about 'business'"—he uncrossed his arms and did air quotes, a gesture he hated—"some other time?"

"Dad, that's what I'm saying. How about tomorrow night?"

* * *

So that was how the party went, and the conversation with Beatrice, and then the conversation with his daughter, but still, Morley wasn't certain how he'd ended up at a university Starbucks with the mall girls. He'd never said yes to this meeting.

Last night he'd told his wife about it as they got ready for bed.

"Hmm," she'd said and spat out her toothpaste. "It can't hurt, right?"

"You're saying to humor them."

"I'm saying to listen to them." She slipped her toothbrush into the holder. He stood gripping his. "What kind of business do they have in mind?" she asked.

"I don't know. This is a pipe dream. You realize that."

"Maybe it is." She smiled at him in the mirror and leaned closer to examine her crow's feet. "But sometimes people surprise you."

Morley put his toothbrush in his mouth and brushed for a few seconds. Then he tossed it on the counter and left the bathroom.

When his wife came into the bedroom she whispered, "Hon? I'm having a little déjà vu. Are we fighting?"

He didn't answer.

She got into bed. "Ah, the bathroom, a scene of so much domestic drama."

He still didn't answer. He knew he was being petulant.

"I'm kidding," his wife said. She touched his foot with hers. "Honestly, though, you might consider taking her seriously once in a while."

He sniffed and she said, "Oh Morley, I'm sorry. I don't want to overstep my bounds. She's not my daughter. But she's yours and, well, she's Rita's. Do you think Rita would want you to hear her out?"

At the sound of that name—right out loud, twice, from his wife's lips—Morley shuddered. It was a relief to hear it, as though something had been admitted.

"I love you," his wife said.

"I know," Morley answered.

"Oh, the romance."

"I mean—"

"It's okay, sweetheart. I know you love me."

"I do," he said, because it was true.

* * *

He loved his wife, and he loved his daughter, but sometimes he nearly forgot he loved them. Rita had been gone six years and the grief persisted, this obliterating grief that made him forget his current life. He couldn't hold everything at once, Rita and his grief plus his wife and daughter and all the ways he'd supposedly moved on. The grief was only intermittent now, but it seemed to grow more acute, not less. He would shut down periodically and forget he loved his family. He didn't know what of this they perceived.

So even though Morley wasn't certain how he'd ended up spending twenty-five dollars on coffee drinks for the mall girls and sitting on a stool at a tall table with them, he was determined to listen to his daughter and her friends. He would hear them out.

They beamed at him, the two blonds with dark roots, Sophie and Alison. Plus Beatrice, who wavered between a glare and a smirk. And his daughter, Chloe, thirty years old and six years motherless, a community college graduate and the unofficial leader of this pack of mall girls.

They weren't indistinguishable. Morley made himself pay attention. Beatrice had her dark red hair, and Sophie was quite tall. Alison bore an interesting scar that ran from the base of her thumb to her wrist. Morley touched his own wrist.

"All right," he said. "What do you want to talk about?" He took a sip of coffee and did not pull on his sleeve. This morning after he got out of the shower he'd found another altered outfit waiting on his bed.

The girls giggled—well, Beatrice didn't giggle; she had committed to one or another withering facial expression—and put the straws of their espresso milkshakes in their mouths. Alison nudged Chloe, who rolled her eyes and set down her drink.

"Okay," she said, "we don't have a, you know, pitch yet or anything, but what we're thinking is a sort of full-service lifestyle stop."

"Mm-hmm." Morley had no idea what that meant.

"Like, hair and nails and spa things, massages and whatever." That was Sophie, who slouched and had blue eyes. "Plus a shop with clothes and jewelry made by local artists." She pointed around the table to indicate the "local artists."

"And whatever else we can think of," Alison added. She held her coffee with her scarred hand. "Arts and crafts classes, for instance," she said. "Or yoga, and meditation. Stuff like that."

Chloe piped up. "And maybe a café."

"Okay," Morley said. "That's, uh, quite ambitious." He looked from Sophie (purple nail polish, faint acne) to Alison (incipient double chin) to Chloe, then glanced at Beatrice, who turned from him and then turned back.

"Really, you think?" Beatrice said. "Because it's true we are very ambitious." Her face had gone neutral and Morley became aware of his pulse. "Especially Chloe."

"I don't know about that," Chloe said, and he was pleased to see his daughter crinkle her brow at Beatrice (left eye smaller than the right). "We've all thought a lot about this."

Beatrice couldn't know he'd heard her, when she called after him at the party. No one knew, not his wife or Chloe either. And Rita would never know, though sometimes Morley caught himself believing the dead might watch the living.

He tried to stretch his shoulders inside his shirt but ended up only hunching them. "What have you done so far?" he asked the girls.

No one wanted to go ahead and admit "nothing," apparently, because there was a cacophony of hedging and objecting and throat-clearing. While they scrambled for euphemisms—*We're still in the early stages, We're just brainstorming so far*—Morley scanned the place, the university students bowed over laptops and clumped in study groups, and wondered what they saw when they looked at his table, which they weren't doing, in fact, but what would they see, if they did look?

Finally, Beatrice's voice rose above the others'. "We've done quite a lot of research," she said. The girls stopped talking and stared at her. "And it's important to us to consult with many different kinds of experts, anyone who'd have useful knowledge, like about marketing, or sales, or, for example, accounting—"

"All right," Morley said. "Fine. But you've got a lot of work to do." And he let forth a monologue about business plans and credit and capital. He was no business professional, but this was elementary stuff. He asked them if they'd thought about where to house this business and where the clients were going to come from and what their competition looked like and how the thing was going to be run among the four of them, all of whom had degrees in fashion design, right? So who was going to do everything else?

And the whole time he was thinking, *I love you, Chloe, I love you, I love you*. It was a mantra and a reminder and a way for him to keep his volume down and his tone of voice in check.

"Listen, girls," he said, winding up, "it's not altogether clear what you expect me to tell you, but you have a good deal of investigation and basic groundlaying to tackle. Do you understand?" *I love my daughter*, he thought.

He got some nods and mumbling in return, and some sheepish smiles and shrugs, and then without looking at him Chloe started an exodus to the bathroom that, at some point in the comings and goings and gathering of purses and keys, left him alone at the table with Beatrice.

"That was kinda harsh," Beatrice said.

Morley took a sip of coffee and eyed her over the rim of the cup. This girl, what the hell did she want from him? "Do you think I was wrong about anything?" he asked.

"No, actually. No. What you said was helpful. Which was the whole point." She paused, as though to let that sink in, and Morley held her gaze.

She went on. "It's just that Chloe is. . . sort of a visionary. This is her idea. She's really smart, Mr. Otis, and she's been super motivating to all of us."

"Really?" Morley wondered what his daughter was like at school. How had she gotten this following?

"We know we have a lot of work to do. No one's gonna quit their job or anything."

"Chloe doesn't have a job."

Beatrice sighed. "She will. She's looking."

"That's good." He fingered his sleeve and let it go.

"She's really smart."

"You said that." This was dangerous, Morley thought, letting Beatrice tell him about his daughter. He didn't like the way the girl looked at him, squinting through her bangs as though looking for something, something in particular she thought she could see, and that she knew she wouldn't like.

"I mean, Mr. Otis—"

"It's Dr. Otis."

That was petty, he knew, and Beatrice knew it too because she flicked her hand and said, "Whatever."

Morley remembered his daughter's telling him that Beatrice could take a person off guard, so when she said, "Dr. Otis, did you ever think Chloe might be a visionary?" he should have been warned.

Instead, he heard himself say, "Beatrice, I used to wonder if she might be retarded," and the word seemed visible before them, shimmering and hideous in the contrived lambency of Starbucks.

Beatrice opened her mouth and raised her eyebrows into her bangs, and Morley knew there was no recovering from that word so he let her gape at him until she leaned forward and asked, her voice too loud for the cozy coffee hum around them, "For real, what is wrong with you?"

He swallowed and turned his head. He blinked and felt her staring at his profile, and finally, finally the other mall girls came back to the table. He wondered how he would report on this meeting to his wife.

"Thanks for talking to us, Mr. Otis," Sophie said.

"*Dr.* Otis," Beatrice corrected her.

This time it was Morley who wanted to flick his hand and say, "Whatever."

"Anyway," Alison said, "we need to go. My mom called and she's pissed I took her car. But thanks, uh, Dr. Otis. And can you take Beattie home? I think it's more on your way."

"No problem," he told her, and inhaled deeply through his nose. "Good luck."

Sophie and Alison left and Beatrice followed. The three girls clustered at the entrance, and Morley watched them for a few seconds. Surely Beatrice wasn't repeating what he'd said. He looked down at his coffee cup and up again toward the restrooms. Where was his daughter?

Beatrice strode back to the table, and Morley tracked her in his peripheral vision. Behind her he saw the other mall girls wave in his direction and leave.

"You stay here," Beatrice told him, in the same too-loud voice. "I'm going to get Chloe."

Morley stayed for a moment, then he got up and made his way to the door. Outside, he stretched and exhaled—he fairly panted—and was surprised at the strength of his relief to be out of that stifling faux ambiance. He could only hope Beatrice wouldn't tell Chloe what he'd said, and that Chloe would accept an apology for his being "kinda harsh." Then everything would blow over and he could probably manage never to see Beatrice again.

Morley checked his watch. Nearly 8 p.m. They'd been inside Starbucks only half an hour.

The door opened and there were the two girls, looking just fine, he was glad to see, not angry or wounded. Morley stood up straight.

"Oh there you are," Chloe said.

"Chloe, listen." He put his hand on her shoulder and ignored how his sleeve rode up. "I'm sorry. That was a little. . . harsh." He glanced at Beatrice, who was staring down the street, her arms folded across her chest.

"Oh, it's all right." Chloe shrugged his hand off. "You just wanted to watch out for us. I understand."

"Okay. You understand. Good." He looked again at Beatrice, who caught his eye this time and said, "Let's go."

In the car Chloe sat turned around in the passenger seat, chatting to Beatrice in the back about their "full-service lifestyle stop" and what else might go in it, a dance studio, maybe, sewing classes.

Beatrice gave only murmured answers, and Morley couldn't wait to get rid of that affronted presence in the backseat, but Beatrice's place—that is, her mother's place—wasn't "on the way" from Starbucks to his house, so he had to drive out past town a couple of miles to drop the girl off. He was going a bit too fast when he crested a small rise in the road and spied a deer a hundred yards or so ahead.

"Deer!" Chloe said.

Morley slowed the car and followed the grade of the road down a little and then up, and the deer was still there. He stopped, and a few seconds passed before he understood why the animal didn't run away, why it tipped forward at a queer angle, why it was moving but not getting anywhere: its front legs were broken.

"Ohhh!" Morley and Chloe and Beatrice mewled in unison as they watched the frantic animal struggle to stand.

"Someone hit it," Chloe said, and put her face in her hands. "Oh god, I don't want to see this."

"We have to kill it," Beatrice said. "Dr. Otis?" She poked him in the arm. "We have to kill it."

And by "we," she meant he would have to kill it, as the only man and the only real adult.

"Do you have a gun?" she asked.

"No, Beatrice! For heaven's sake." But Morley wished he did have a gun, the only time he'd wished that in his life.

He put the car in park and undid his seatbelt and opened the door, and before he got out he considered running the deer over, finishing the job the last driver had started, or at least pulling the animal off the road.

"Come on!" Beatrice said, and poked his arm again.

"Beattie, it's all right," Chloe told her.

Without looking at either girl, Morley got out and shut the door and walked a few paces closer to the deer, who continued trying and failing to stand. *We want the same thing,* he thought. *We both want you to run away.* And he watched—he couldn't help it—the clattery collapse, collapse, collapse as the animal tested its hooves and fell.

A doe, Morley noted. Small, last year's baby. He could probably hold it, and if he could get one good, deep swipe across its throat, the whole procedure might not be too terrible.

Morley stepped back to the car and opened the passenger door. Chloe still had her face in her hands. He touched her elbow. "There's that Swiss Army knife," he said. It was a knife for slicing cheese at picnics, but it was all he had.

She nodded and opened the glove box and rooted around. "Here."

"Do you need help?" Beatrice asked.

"No," he said, and shut the door.

It took him six steps to reach the deer, and as he walked he observed his heart, how it seemed simultaneously to reach up into his throat and pulse there, and to contract, turn in on itself. He blinked and remembered to breathe and then he knelt by the deer, who rolled one big brown eye at him and stood and collapsed faster.

It was the bone below the knee that was broken, on both legs. The shins and hooves dangled, and Morley was afraid to see any more of the break, so shocking was the appearance of a joint where no joint existed and that useless swinging movement, all connections severed, the brain no longer able to make the body do what it wanted.

So he focused on the animal's side, on its smooth undisturbed fur. "Shh, nice girl, nice girl."

There was no good place to hold a deer, but Morley seized it around the base of its neck with one arm and tried to pull it to his chest. The animal strained against his grip, its front legs still going. He forced its head up with his other hand, the hand that held the knife, but the deer was stronger than it looked, even with the broken legs, and it jerked away and fell off his lap.

"Damn it!" Morley said and pounded his thigh with his fist. "Jesus." He was breathing hard now, kneeling in the road with the headlights of the idling car trained on him. He couldn't imagine how this appeared, a small old man wrestling a deer while two traumatized girls sat in the car.

Morley wasn't sure of his strength anymore and he badly wanted to drag the deer off the road and be done with it, but such cowardice would plague him forever.

"I'm sorry, I'm sorry," he whispered. "I'm so sorry."

On hands and knees, he approached the animal. It rolled its eye at him again, that placid face so disconcerting. If it were human it would have some expression.

It wasn't human, though. It had four legs and a skinny head and a tail. But the deer's size made it difficult to kill; it was big the way humans were big. A suffering squirrel, or even a cat, could be squinted away, but he couldn't avoid seeing this deer.

So he saw it. He saw it as he put his knees and then his whole weight on the animal's side and tried again to force the head up. He opened the knife and stabbed the blade in and cried out. The blood started, and behind him he heard a car door open and Chloe's voice shout, "Dad!"

There was the sound of running, and he struggled to move the blade through tendons and ligaments and the lesser veins, hoping for the jugular. Blood obscured the details of what he exposed, but the deer was alive, still fighting under him. He scraped his hand through its neck.

"Dad."

He shook his head.

"I'll sit on her," Chloe said.

She sat on the deer, straddling it, and pushed Morley off. He crouched over its head and the deer looked at him as he pushed the knife in again and raked and raked.

Finally, he heard Beatrice say, "It stopped moving."

He raised his head and saw her standing behind Chloe, then he and Chloe stood too, and they all watched as the animal bled out. Its neck was a ragged hole and Morley wondered what it was like to die. How tightly bound we are, he thought, encased by skin and furred over.

And he didn't want to, but he thought of Rita, how it was hard for him to look at her when she was dying, to look at cancer as it pushed against the confines of her body. "I'm so sorry," he mumbled, and he looked up at his daughter. She was crying now, her wrists in her eyes.

"It's not your fault," she said.

Then he looked at Beatrice and said again, "I'm sorry."

"I know," she answered.

Morley bent down and pulled the deer into the weeds by the side of the road. He touched Chloe with his elbow, and as they walked to the car he let her cross to the driver's side. She got in and opened the passenger door, and when Morley slid onto the seat, his bloody hands raised, she said, "Here, I found a plastic bag."

He dropped the knife in and she leaned over to fasten his seatbelt and pull his door shut. Then she turned around. "Oh, Beattie. Ohhhh."

"I'm fine," Beatrice said, and sniffed. "I'll be fine."

Chloe put the car in drive. As they rolled over the bloody spot on the pavement, Morley closed his eyes. There was nothing more to see. Dusk had fallen.

"Poor old Dad," Chloe said, and tapped him on the knee. She lowered her voice. "Poor old Dad."

"Poor old Dad," he echoed.

When he and Rita were thirty-eight she gave him an ultimatum: "I am too old to deliberate any longer, Morley. I'm getting pregnant, and I'll do it with you or without you. Take your pick." He'd picked with.

When the car stopped, Morley opened his eyes. Chloe got out and hugged Beatrice and the two girls stood talking, then Chloe got back in and rolled down the window.

Beatrice leaned over and looked at them. "Drive safely," she said. "I mean, that was harsh. Will you two be all right?"

BABY TRUE TOT

When the kitty died, Mamie Chen bought a baby doll. Baby True Tot.

"Baby Give Me the Creeps," Richard Tyler said. "Baby Freak Me the Fuck Out. I think this forebodes a weird, bad situation." Then he looked at Mamie Chen holding the doll and thought *mi vida* and *mi amor*.

There were staff conversations about the doll, and there were resident conversations, and they were pretty much the same.

"Maybe she misses the kitty."

"Maybe she had a child and lost it."

"Maybe she's adopted."

"But her last name is 'Chen.'"

"So maybe she was adopted by some Chinese people here. That could happen."

It embarrassed everyone when Mamie brought the doll places like the grocery store or the mall. The staff didn't like to hold it while she tried things on.

And for the residents, these group outings—with the huge purchases and the tax-exempt credit card embossed with the facility's name—were bad enough. It was hard both to keep your distance and not get lost, and the doll increased their cognitive dissonance. Everyone thought of bolting. But then what? None of them knew. Not a one knew how to live normal.

Mamie Chen hung on to the doll not so much like a baby as like a purse or an oxygen tank, something she meant to keep hold of but that didn't require much of her. More than once someone had lunged for the thing when it looked as though she would drop it.

"That Muppet is smack-dab in the uncanny valley," Richard Tyler said. *Mein Liebchen.*

Residents could buy whatever they wanted with their own money, so when Mamie saw the ad for Baby True Tot in a magazine at the dentist's after the kitty died, Sherrie said yeah, sure, they could get some money orders for it. Mamie had the cash for three payments of $49.95.

Sherrie quit soon after they made the order, and no one could have guessed what Mamie would do with the doll. Whenever anyone asked her—*Why do you bring it to the grocery store? Why do you take it on walks?*—Mamie answered, "The magazine said, 'So true to life, you'll be tempted to take her with you everywhere.'"

Baby True Tot was stuck in a belly-down position, furry blond head to one side, arms out. When Mamie held it, it appeared to praise the lord or raise the roof. Its eyes were perpetually open, and its mouth too. Sometimes she set it on a shelf and admired the undulating asymmetry of the doll against the flat of the wood.

Mamie overheard some staff agree that Baby True Tot was "creepy." She didn't disagree, but they were missing the point. She knew she might be missing the point too, but she was open to temptation.

They got a new kitty and named it Mahler, and everyone waited to see if Mamie would abandon the doll for the cat. She didn't, and Mahler sat with her and Baby True Tot sometimes, the doll on its front or its back or its side, or with the animal huddled between its beseeching arms.

Richard was running out of tongues. *Mon amour. Mio amore.* There were others that required transliteration, but Richard didn't trust transliteration. So he'd stick with the Romance languages, plus the outlandish German, which could lead, if he weren't careful, to Dutch and even the Scandinavian tongues—and there was also Eastern Europe.

He would mix it up a bit with *mi vida*. He liked that one best, the little turn, the slant-wise way of saying "I love you." *Ay, mi vida*. My own life.

But after finalizing all of that, Richard woke in the early morning thinking about Mandarin and Cantonese. Where was Mamie from? It was a question with profound implications.

Richard Tyler was from Scranton. Mamie Chen was from Phoenix, before her family moved to Schenectady. Baby True Tot was from Ashton-Drake. Most of the staff were from the university. Mahler was from the Humane Society, whence the old cat, Crinklefoot, had come as well.

And they'd all ended up here. What were the chances?

Mamie liked to touch Baby True Tot's eyes, or, the indented spots on the thing called Baby True Tot that were portrayals of eyes. They were blue and black and white and paint and circles. Under her thumbs lay the smooth vinyl, its color so carefully applied as to leave no texture.

She was tempted to take the doll with her everywhere, so she did. She knew it wasn't a baby. It was a made thing with a purpose that eluded and fascinated her. Baby True Tot was molded to lie on a shelf, not to be taken everywhere, but maybe this contradiction was part of the dollmaker's statement.

There were people here who saw the thing called Baby True Tot and saw the thing called Mamie Chen and saw the thing called Richard Tyler and accepted them all, and the acceptance was obvious and remarkable. Richard asked himself questions that were unanswerable but essential, and sometimes he fairly trembled at their enormity. Not really, but he wanted to tremble; he wanted to weep.

After a while a rift developed among the staff. Some saw the doll as a hindrance to Mamie's progress. Others figured there were worse things, and what was "progress" anyway?

Both groups felt vindicated when, at dinner one night, Richard Tyler suggested it was most unsanitary for Mamie to hold the doll on her lap under the tablecloth. Then he belched and let a mouthful of food fall onto his plate, and when Leonard—who was in the "what was progress?" camp—said it would be helpful if Richard could remember his table manners, Richard let the plate fly in a slow and lovely arc until it hit the wall but didn't shatter because it was Corelle. And later he had to be taken down and given his emergency med, which they got him to swallow by massaging his throat with swift downward strokes the way you'd do a cat.

Mamie considered Richard to be right or left of her radar, a person she couldn't quite look at. This would hurt him, so she never said it, just stepped one way or the other when he came at her. Sometimes these steps made her think of dancing, which was not an impression she wanted to give.

She'd hold the doll straight out from her body, like a warning, and she could see Richard plotting an end run, but Baby True Tot was an impervious force.

What was temptation, and what was gained by not giving in? What was love? Richard asked himself over and over because there was nothing for him to do but love Mamie Chen, who had found god in a baby doll and ended up where he'd ended up and nowhere else. She was crazy in a way similar enough to the way he was crazy that they lived in a house together in a semi-desirable neighborhood with normal people for neighbors whose proximity could be thrilling.

Richard didn't mind words like "crazy" and "normal" and used them freely, sometimes to goad the staff, who were aware, but dimly, that residents knew things they didn't. College was useful; Richard had gone to college too, and it was a pure, sweet time in life, but who could know what threshold? Twenty-one had been his breakdown year. He liked to call it his break-*out* year, a little joke, as though he'd arrived in an important way. Which, of course, he had. All along his body and brain had hurtled toward the sudden turn, and afterward his life lay at a right angle to where it had been.

Richard didn't really think the situation with Baby True Tot would turn into a weird, bad situation, but it was going to turn into something. Then they would be different, not unlike the way the whole world was, every new and portentous second, entirely not the same.

If Mamie got up for a drink while watching TV, she would set Baby True Tot in her place until she got back. Baby True Tot started sitting in at card games too, and Mamie's opponents learned to deal her out.

One morning she woke early to put Baby True Tot in her chair at the breakfast table and left to walk by herself to McDonald's. Residents weren't supposed to do that, but her defense would be, "I'm an adult." Staff were always saying so: you're *adults*. They said it with special passion.

Mamie left the doll at the scene of half-done chores, in her bed when she'd claimed to be sick, in the bathroom with the door shut and the shower running. In the middle of activity therapy she stood up from the table covered in pots of glue and cut-up magazines, put Baby True Tot in her seat, and walked out the front door. A couple of staff followed her. "Hey!" one yelled. Mamie strode away. "You have to come back."

Mamie turned. "I know," she said. "I will." And she did, after going twice around the block.

"We're not fooled," Leonard said later. "The doll is not your stand-in."

"I'm not trying to fool you," Mamie answered. "Baby True Tot is white." She knew she couldn't make Leonard see anything, but she smiled and hoped they might enjoy some companionable silence.

"You can't run away," Leonard said.

"I'm not."

"Why do you do it?"

"That's an interesting name, Leonard, for a young person. Was it your grandfather's?"

"No. Mamie, it worries us when you just take off."

"Then I'll tell you from now on. Or I'll leave a note."

"I've gone" was the note she left the next time. Richard Tyler found it, propped between Baby True Tot's hands on the dining room table. He read the note and wondered how long he would live here doing—what? He was only forty or so. He could pass, sometimes. It took a lot of effort, but he could comb his hair and stand up straight and not do the things he knew would earn him a takedown. (He knew, he always knew, but takedowns and the events leading to them were out-of-body experiences.)

Mamie had ordered Baby True Tot because she had the money and because she was tempted to, and what better reasons? Now she left the house nearly every day because that was the new thing tempting her. Baby True Tot had opened Mamie Chen to the possibilities of her life. Richard wanted to know what it would take for him.

He put the note in his pocket and picked up Baby True Tot, and in the weight of the doll he felt the weight of Mamie's leaving. But there was no newness in that because—of course, of course—he always missed her. She would come back, or she wouldn't, and it could not make any difference for Richard Tyler.

Mamie did come back, and she made no mention of the filching of her note or of Baby True Tot's lying perhaps slightly askew on the table. She only picked the doll up by its elbow and went to her room, and no one dared reprimand her. She was beyond all reprimanding, having found a portal to her own life.

At age eleven, Mamie was on a swing in the backyard, swinging high, and she realized she could reach the newly restrung clothesline with her mouth. The force yanked a few teeth out and bloodied her whole jaw, which was sore for weeks. Several months later, her father was transferred from Arizona to New York.

There was no cause and effect, but these events defined being eleven and constituted the period by which her parents measured the past and future. After eleven, everything would look familiar, the risk-taking that stretched into Mamie's teens and adulthood, and that, looking back, defined her early years as well. She'd pressed her forehead to cacti, made fists around knives, tried to pop her eyeball out of her head to see if it would dangle, ate any mushroom she found growing anywhere.

Later, in New York, she drank and used and slept around, which devastated her parents but seemed still within the zone of teenage rebellion. Then her mother came home to find the power cut and her daughter naked and strung out on the bathroom floor. A hairdryer floated in the bathtub. When Mamie came to, she explained she'd gotten out of the tub first, then plugged in the hairdryer, turned it on, and tossed it in the water to see what would happen.

That was more than twenty years ago, and despite the time and her meds she still felt the teetering that might or might not lead her to slice off her tongue or jump from the roof or—if she had a gun, say she had a gun and knew how to use it—insert one bullet and spin the cylinder.

It wasn't that Mamie wanted to die, per se, but she was enthralled by how quickly a person could cross from the ordinary to the spectacular.

Richard was hardly surprised when the thing that happened was this: Mamie left and he—suffering from the aftermath of a takedown and his emergency med, which fuzzed his brain—combed his hair, took Baby True Tot from its spot by the front door, and followed her.

He carried Baby True Tot as though it could watch over his shoulder, and he wondered if he appeared to be a man carrying his child, or a man chasing the woman he loved with her doll.

He caught up to Mamie at a crosswalk. She turned and Richard held out Baby True Tot.

"Mamie," he said. "Mi amor."

Mamie didn't know what he meant. "What do you want?" she said and looked at the light. It said DON'T WALK.

"Where do you go, Mamie?"

"Go away. And take that back." She gestured to Baby True Tot. "Put it where I left it."

"Mi amor," Richard repeated. "Mein Liebchen." He shook Baby True Tot for emphasis.

This time Mamie caught some meaning in his syllables. She reached for Baby True Tot, ready to snatch it from Richard, but he let go and Mamie jerked the doll away so it swung behind her and she almost dropped it.

She recovered and held Baby True Tot by one arm. She twisted the arm back and forth. From her peripheral vision she saw the light change again.

"Go," she said.

Richard wondered if anyone driving past would mistake the doll for a real baby. Imagine their horror. So true to life.

The meds Mamie took now mitigated her impulses, but she still noted what tempted her: jump into traffic, push Richard into traffic, at the very least throw Baby True Tot into traffic. That would be a spectacular end to Baby True Tot.

DON'T WALK said the light, and Mamie hoisted Baby True Tot to her hip as though the doll weighed more than it did. She stepped off the curb and paused. Traffic zipped past. Then she lifted Baby True Tot above her head and WALKed. Cars halted. There was abruptness, the stomping of brake pedals and the music of horns, but everyone waited for Mamie to make her way.

Richard Tyler was as mesmerized as the rest of them. Soon the police would be here because surely someone was on a phone saying a woman had walked into the road carrying a baby over her head, or maybe just a doll; it was hard to tell, but still, it might be a baby so hurry.

Richard looked at Mamie Chen and thought of Moses. Here she was on the precipice of so much—arrest, violence, death—and she WALKed across the street.

When she reached the other side she turned, as though to witness what she'd wrought, and traffic started again. She didn't smile and she didn't look at Richard Tyler. He was a man who could pass sometimes, but not today, and he thought, *Ay, ay, ay, mi amor.* Mi vida. My life.

Mamie turned back around and took off, grasping Baby True Tot by the neck, and Richard waited until the light said WALK, then he stepped into the street. He made his careful way, and the light counted down the seconds: 15, 14, 13, 12. He would not pursue Mamie Chen—she could never ever love him. He would only go where she was going.

ORDINARY CIRCUMSTANCES

My kid likes going to the doctor. I can't explain it. She greets him like he's Santa Claus, and she's sitting there shivering in her yellow socks and her kitten underpants and a paper gown with clowns on it. The doctor—I like him, he was my pediatrician—is this old guy with a bow tie and suspenders. He's got one hell of a head of silver hair. His hairline hasn't moved in decades (mine's been moving since I was twenty-two; now I'm forty), and I contemplate it as he talks to my daughter.

"Lillian, how are you feeling? I'm very glad to see you."

"I'm glad to see you too," Lil says, grinning.

He sits on his rolling stool and peers at her, and she looks down at him from her perch on the exam table.

"She's had a cough," I say, and they ignore me.

Lil coughs, and he brings his stethoscope to his ears. "Let's see what we can hear."

She corrects him. "Let's *hear* what we can hear."

He tips an imaginary hat to her and winks, then slips the metal disc under the top of her paper gown. He turns his head my way and listens. He's not looking at me. He's concentrating. He moves the metal disc and listens some more.

Lillian is fine. She's had a cough for two days, is all. She's seven and healthy, though small. This is a well-child visit, and she'll get a flu shot and have a nice chat with her friend Dr. Phillips.

He moves his metal disc again, and my kid leans forward.

"Lillian," the doctor whispers, "don't hold your breath."

She giggles and looks at me and I wink too, and then she turns serious and remembers to breathe for several seconds.

Everybody's quiet, and Lil says, "Are you listening to my heart now?"

The doctor says yes.

She's quiet again.

"Breathe, Lillian," he says.

"Can you hear God?" she asks him. "In my heart?"

"Lil—" I start. This kind of stuff comes from her mother. I can just hear her. *God is in your heart, Lillian.*

But Dr. Phillips interrupts. "Well," he says, and looks at me. I shrug.

"Not literally," he tells her. He takes off the stethoscope. "Do you know what that means, 'literally'?"

She shakes her head.

"It means that what I hear with my ears is your heart beating and your lungs breathing. So I don't hear God the way I hear your insides, or the way you hear me now."

It's a pretty good answer. I'd have been tempted just to tell her no.

He keeps going. "But here in the middle of your chest, where your heart is—" He taps his own chest, and he taps Lil's. "Sometimes it seems to people that they feel happiness there, or love. Or they put their hands over their hearts when they hear the national anthem, because they want to show it's important. Do you know the national anthem?"

She nods. It's news to me.

Dr. Phillips puts his hand over his heart, and Lillian does too. My tiny daughter—last time we were here she was in the thirtieth percentile for height and weight—she puts her tiny hand on her tiny chest and turns to me, and I put my hand on my chest too, and it's like we're all going to break out in "O say can you see. . . ?"

"So if people say God is in their hearts, what they mean is they have a special feeling and it seems like it comes from right here." He holds his hand there a moment before placing it on his knee, and Lillian and I drop our hands too.

"Okay," she says. "I can feel it."

"Great," the doctor answers, and he gets on with it. He looks in her eyes and ears and nose, and taps her knees and does all the usual stuff, and when he takes out his chart and compares her numbers we learn she's inched up to the thirty-fifth percentile.

"That's wonderful, Lillian, you're growing," Dr. Phillips tells her. "You're not a large child, but you're a healthy one." She grins and grins, and he shakes her hand and shakes mine—"A lovely daughter you have, Jeremy"—and bows on his way out, and when the nurse comes in to do the flu shot, Lil wants me to note she is very brave and it doesn't even hurt that much.

When we leave she takes my hand. "You're a wiseacre," she tells me. "You're a real weisenheimer."

"You're a knucklehead," I answer.

"You're a knucklehead and a bonehead. And a weisenheimer."

Weisenheimer is her favorite.

"You're a ninnyhammer," I say.

"You're a scallywag."

We go on like that, and I take her back to school. When she gets out of the car, she shouts, "You're a nincompoop!" and I blow her a kiss.

"Lillian's fine," I tell my wife later, over the phone. "Tiny, but not as tiny."

"That's great," May says. "I thought so. She seems more robust."

"She'll still be a runt."

"Maybe she's a late bloomer."

I doubt it. Lil did things early—teethe, walk, talk—and May's people and my people are not impressive physical specimens.

I listen to May breathing. Maybe I can't even really hear her, but I know she's there, breathing. She's at her parents' restaurant, and what I for sure do hear is a lot of clatter and shouting. It's dinnertime, and I resist asking my wife whether she's coming to our house after.

But I throw her a bone. "Lil asked the doctor if he could hear God while he was listening to her heart."

"Ohhhh," May says. "That is so sweet. What did he say?"

What the doctor said reminds me now of *Yes, Virginia, there is a Santa Claus*. "He said not literally but sort of, if you feel it."

It's a terrible answer, and May is quiet.

"Lil said she feels it."

My wife exhales. "I love that," she says. But I'm not sure how to respond right away so she says, "I know you don't love it."

"Honey, I'm just telling you."

We both hear how weird that sounds, me calling her honey, and it makes me sad that it sounds so weird.

May comes around sometimes. She brings us fried rice and vegetables from the restaurant, or sweet and sour chicken, or moo shu pork. Lillian has two twin beds in her room, and when May sleeps there I can barely sleep at all. I lie in our bed and feel like I'm being electrocuted. I don't really know what it's like to be electrocuted, but I'm pretty sure it's exactly like lying in a queen-size bed down the hall from your wife, who hasn't let you touch her in months. Just try telling me electrocution isn't like that.

I married the only Chinese woman in northern Michigan. That's not really true. It's just a stupid thing I like to say. There are two other Asian kids in Lil's school, actually, and two black kids (one's biracial, like her), and a handful of Latino kids, and some Native Americans. Mostly they're white, but she's not the only one who isn't.

Lillian appears to take our new precarious living situation in stride. She's happy to see May when she comes but doesn't ask what the hell is going on when she doesn't. And she visits her grandparents like normal and lives in the same house with me and goes to school and seems just fine. But I fear this can't last. Plus, May's gotten religion and I'm a jerk for being skeptical, especially since it started when her cousin's kid was dying of leukemia.

Kids aren't supposed to die of leukemia anymore. You hear cure rates like sixty, seventy percent and you think, well, that covers this kid, then. But Albert ended up in that smaller percent for reasons that are incomprehensible. Besides the cancer he was healthy, which sounds nuts. Oh, he's got a strong heart and lungs? That's just terrific, but when the cancer gets him it's going to stop his top-notch organs too.

May and her cousin are pretty tight, and when Albert was diagnosed her cousin somehow got tangled up with this cuckoo Christian witch doctor who talked about "energy" and the light of Christ and giving Jesus your burden, which was harmless in the sense that she didn't suggest stopping treatment or anything, but listening to this woman added up to a lot of wasted time and wasted *energy*. I didn't meet her, but I heard about her because May fell for it too.

When Albert died, almost a year ago, May told Lillian he'd gone to heaven. Lillian asked me if that was true, so I told her, and here I quote myself, "Yep."

I couldn't say, "No, Lil. Your cousin's nothing anymore. He's meat now, and he's going in the ground," but neither could I muster any enthusiasm for heaven. "Yep" was good enough for Lillian, though. It wasn't good enough for May.

And that's when our marriage started to trickle away. I couldn't comfort my wife in the way she wanted. She says I was (am) disdainful of her faith. But it's not so much disdain as bewilderment.

Before Albert died, May believed in God in an offhand way. God was a comforting idea. She's second generation, but her parents came here as kids, so they're all used to the American ambivalent/secular approach to religious holidays. We'd acknowledge Jesus at Christmas and Easter, but the main show was the trees and the eggs and the magical gift-givers.

And she'd do prayers with Lil, "Now I lay me down to sleep," and Lillian would go along in her tiny singsong voice, "If I should die before I wake, I pray the Lord my soul to take."

May would do prayers, we'd read a couple of stories, and Lil and I would exchange a few old-timey insults:

"You're a slugabed."

"You're a jackanapes."

"You're a clodhopper."

"You're a weisenheimer."

Then we'd turn out the light, and several nights a week I'd seduce my wife in our big queen-size bed. That was back when prayers were more like nursery rhymes and God was a comforting idea and none of us had ever been to a ten-year-old's funeral.

Besides May's newly fervent belief and unpredictable habitating, though, she is a solid person and a good mother. She sees Lillian a lot. She comes here and takes her to the restaurant and her parents' house and even my parents' house. She shows up for school things and helps at the restaurant even while working thirty hours as a dental hygienist. But sometimes I come home and find her doing laundry or weeding in the front, and that stuff just kills me.

The fact that May is still invested in our household does seem encouraging. Her paychecks go into our joint account, and she hasn't mentioned separate accounts or getting her own place (she stays at her parents', I assume, when she isn't in Lillian's extra bed) or divorce.

I love May. Jesus Christ, what am I supposed to do with that? I can't turn it off, and that is the cruelty of desire. By desire I don't mean just sex. I mean longing, like *soul-longing*, if that's not ridiculous. I do all the usual things, take care of Lil, go to work, keep the house from falling apart, but for months it's like I've been screaming. There are two parallel Jeremys: one carries on and the other one can't stop screaming. That's probably how Albert's parents feel too.

It was Dr. Phillips who sent Albert to the children's hospital in Grand Rapids, where they diagnosed him. What a job. I wonder why he's still doing it. He must be seventy.

When Lil had strep throat six months ago, he said to me, "Ah, Jeremy, I've thought about your family every day since young Albert died." I bet if I asked him how many of his patients have died as children he'd be able to tell me right off. But when you go into pediatrics, I suppose you know what you're signing up for.

So anyway, for reasons having to do with wanting to please May and wanting to keep her on the phone, I tell her about Lillian feeling God in her heart, even though it worries me some. What the heck does Lil think she feels?

After May and I recover from how weird it is when I call her "honey" she says she'll come by that evening, but it's Friday so she might be late at the restaurant. I have that familiar jubilant feeling followed immediately by that familiar despairing feeling, and that's pretty much my life these days. Double Jeremys: screaming and getting on with it.

It's six o'clock and I go find Lil in her room and suggest we go to the beach. In September it's still nice up here. You might not want to swim, but I'll sit on the sand and watch Lake Michigan and let Lil run around any day. We even go in winter, with hats and coats. It's crazy how dangerous the lake is. Summer and winter people go out on piers when they shouldn't. They get blown off and bash their heads on rocks and drown.

At the beach Lil wants to play on the monkey bars and swings close to the parking lot. I let her do that for ten minutes or so, then hustle her down toward the water. Lake Michigan, how to explain it? The first time I saw the Atlantic Ocean, I said, "It looks like the Great Lakes." People who've never been here don't get it. They pay more attention to the word "lakes" than the word "great," and they picture a reedy, shallow pond. Some of the lakeshore is rocky, but here there's approximately one million yards of white sand from the parking lot to the water. It's beautiful. I could look at it forever.

At the shore Lillian digs in the sand and shrieks when the surf grabs her. By the time she tells me she's hungry it's dusky and she's soaked through and shivering. I make her stand still and tolerate a brisk brushing-off of wet sand, which is mostly fruitless, and we head home. I don't mention her mother to her, but when we get to the house the lights are on, and when I open the door there's that warm, rice-y smell. I think of May's parents' food as one of the major sensory accompaniments of our marriage.

"Mama!" Lil squeals when the door opens. "Noodles!"

She wriggles out of her wet, sandy pants in the entryway, and I toss them over the porch railing before shutting the door behind us. May comes out of the kitchen wiping her hands on her jeans. Lil runs to her.

"Oh, you're so cold!" my wife says. "Let's get you in the bath." She looks at me. "Jeremy, you could put the food in the oven to keep it warm."

Every last thing she says to me, I hope to hear encouragement in it. But I'm not supposed to question her coming and going while she—I don't even know what. Decides whether to leave for good, I guess. So I wait for her. I sit in our house drinking a beer and warming our dinner while she bathes our kid, and I wait for her.

When they come back to the kitchen Lillian's in a fluffy yellow nightgown that makes her look like a black-capped duckling, and she's flushed and dewy from the bath. We grin at each other as though a warmed-up meal of Chinese food after trips to the doctor and the beach is the most delightful thing. Which it is.

It's all familiar to her, this house, the food, the beach, Dr. Phillips—what happens when he dies?—May and me. Sometimes in my desperation I forget that if May leaves me for real it will hurt Lil too.

I have this thought that's both comforting and disturbing. If May leaves I'll feel like killing myself but I won't do it because I have Lillian. And not killing myself will benefit other people too: my parents, and May's parents, I suppose, and the people who work for me. But nobody needs me the way Lil does, so without her I might seriously be tempted to walk into Lake Michigan.

We have this small table in our kitchen with one side pushed against the wall, so there's room for just three chairs. A couple of years ago, before Albert was diagnosed, we were thinking of having another kid, but now my focus is on preventing attrition. Three of us seems perfect. May and I are only children too.

After May gets the food she sits and clasps her hands and so does Lillian. I put mine in my lap to wait for them.

"Dear Lord," my wife starts, "thank you for this food." She gives thanks for our health and for God's loving embrace of cousin Albert in heaven.

Maybe you could have just left him here, God, I think. This is the kind of thing that makes me impatient with May's new Christian devotion. Albert died and it sucks, and it isn't part of some plan, because what a shitty plan that would be. So great job, God, taking care of him in heaven, but that would be plan B. Actually, that's plan Z.

May wraps it up, and Lillian ends with her usual "And thank you God for our happy family. A-men!"

You hear that, May? Our happy family. A-men!

"Tell Mom about Dr. Phillips today, Lil."

"I'm growing!"

"That's wonderful. I knew you were."

"Me too," Lillian says. "I knew it."

I smile and catch May's eye, and I want to wink but it seems too flirty. She smiles back, though.

So dinner is fine, and predictable at this point. May and I are courteous, familiar if not friendly, and Lil chatters and seems thrilled to have us both here.

When she gets tired she reaches for me. May says she'll clean up and I carry Lil to the bathroom, coax her to brush her teeth, and carry her to bed. I lie down with her, on top of the covers, squishing myself against the wall. Fatherhood is this lovely, ordinary thing, and sometimes I feel like I want to sort of rest in it, snuggle up to it, like I'm snuggling Lillian now. I used to feel that way about marriage too.

May and I cannot be said to have exciting lives, but I liked to tell her we had an epic love story in ordinary circumstances. It became a thing: one of us would say, "Epic love story," and the other would answer, "Ordinary circumstances." It was one of the first things I said to her after Lillian was born.

When I wake up my arm is violently asleep, still pressed to the wall. I sit and scoot to the end of Lil's bed and lift my dead arm into my lap with my other arm. Lying in the second twin bed, perpendicular to Lillian's, is my wife. This is the first time in months we've slept in the same room.

I can make out the contrast of her black hair on the white pillow, so I stare at that. What will she say if she wakes? My arm is prickling back to life, and I wonder how long I'd have to cut off the circulation to do real damage. Probably a long time, but it's weird and scary all the easy ways to injure yourself, cuts and burns, stopping blood flow, falling off the pier. Getting cancer. Walking into the lake.

It's maybe creepy, staring at May, and the fact that looking at my wife might be creepy starts to piss me off, which is dangerous. When I get angry she seems further away.

I don't want to be creepy, so I get up and head to the bathroom, where the clock says 3:33. I consider all kinds of crazy things for the middle of the night, taking a walk, making coffee, looking at my phone for no good reason. I should go back to sleep, but I decide to take a shower first. It's a comfortable place to cry and not as lonely as our bed.

In the morning—real morning, not 3 a.m.—Lil wakes me up.

"Get up, ya milquetoast."

She's leaning on my chest in her yellow nightgown, a cheerful morning duck.

"Mom's making breakfast."

I can smell it.

I pull on some pants. It seems—I don't know, presumptuous?—to walk around in my underwear in front of May.

There's coffee and scrambled eggs and pancakes, made by my wife, here in our house. Ordinary circumstances.

She's showered and dressed. She keeps some clothes in Lil's closet. Sometimes I go in there and look at them. There are clothes in our bedroom closet still too, but I guess those she's abandoned.

After breakfast Lil scampers off, and May and I sit at the table with our coffee cups, not looking at each other. I swear I start to blush. My face and neck get hot and I put my coffee down, and May says, "I talked to Julie yesterday."

Julie is her cousin, Albert's mom.

"They want to have a little service, like a celebration of life."

Today is September 30. Albert died October 7 last year. This year he would have been a sixth-grader.

"I thought a celebration of life was a funeral."

"I don't know. Something, then. A ritual."

And just like that we're both irritated. The way we've been with each other over this almost-year has evolved. Or devolved. First there was a lot of careful discussion about religion and why May didn't always stay here, and then a lulled period of painstaking courtesy, and now that is changing to include flares of frustration. Maybe where we're headed next is open hostility.

"Something with the family, an observance. Just—to say we still love him and. . . that we're okay. And he's okay."

She says this like a challenge, but the truth is I don't think Albert's not okay. Death isn't the worst thing. I just don't think he's anything anymore. I can't help it. I can't talk myself into belief.

"Also, Julie's pregnant."

"Wow."

"Right?"

I hope May is thinking about what I'm thinking about: Julie and Carl having sex. Not in a gross way, but the fact of it. Albert's parents had sex, and we're just Albert's mom's cousin and her husband. I wish May and I were a comfort to each other, and it hits me that if she still loved me it would be too hard for her to stay away. She would feel electrocuted the way I do.

Or maybe not. If she didn't love me she would get the hell out of here. Millions of times I've thought *I can't stand this any longer*. And then I stand it some more.

"Will you come? To Albert's—whatever?"

"Of course."

"I should go. I told my parents I'd help with lunch."

"I'll clean up."

"I want to come get Lillian later."

I nod.

And she's off.

May and I met eleven years ago. She's four years younger, so we were never in high school together, and then I went to college and she cooked at the restaurant and did the dental hygiene thing at the community college.

This is a small city, but there was no reason for us to be in each other's orbit until her car started making a weird knocking sound. I got a BA in philosophy, but I also know about cars, so I came back here and worked with my dad and got certified, and a few years after that we started phasing him out so I could take over his shop.

I'm not a big guy, but I've been told I'm good-looking, baldness and all, and I think I cut some kind of figure for May when she came in, panicked about her car. She probably expected an older fat guy. She probably expected my dad. But it was me who came out from the back, breathless and holding a wrench. You know, it's a type. She noticed.

And I noticed. May is a small woman, but she has a steeliness too. That day her eyes were kind of wild, and she looked so serious. It was the seriousness I noted first. There was a second of recognition between us, with sex bound up in it, then a second of embarrassment, and then I asked what I could do for her.

That was the start of our epic love story.

The knocking turned out to be the end of her engine, and I helped her sell the car for parts and pick out a new car. To say thank you, she opened the restaurant one Sunday evening, when they were normally closed. She cooked for me, no one else there, and later I went home with her, to this apartment she had over top of a storefront downtown.

For a year we went to the beach in all seasons and ate Chinese food and had a lot of sex, and then I asked her father for her hand. I felt weird about it, like can't she make her own decisions? But he loved it. He was so excited I feared he'd tell her before I could, so I went right to her apartment and when she opened the door I said, "Marry me." We raced to her bedroom and only after did I remember the ring. She still wears it, and her wedding ring too. But they seem incidental.

This can't be all about God and Albert, though I might never know. If she finds her way back to me, I will swallow my curiosity. I will swallow it every day like some huge, dry pill.

Albert's funeral was at the beach, on a cold, sunny day. It was windy, and the minister had this crummy wireless microphone. Lillian wore her winter coat and hat, and halfway through she climbed into my lap. She put her lips to my ear and asked, "What is he saying?"

I moved my lips to her ear. "He's saying we all loved Albert very much."

She laid her cheek on my shoulder, then lifted her head again. "What else?"

I didn't know. There was wind and a drone of word-like sounds, and from some yards away the surf, which didn't help, but before I could come up with a gentle and believable answer, Lil said, "Mommy's crying."

I looked at my wife. She had a handkerchief over her nose and mouth, pinned there with a gloved hand, and her torso bobbed in an odd way that took me a second to recognize as sobbing. Her parents were on one side of her, and Lillian and I on the other, but there was something contained and private about her grief that I was both afraid to disturb and afraid to let her get lost in. It seemed—honestly, and as sad as the situation was—out of all proportion.

Holding Lil, I moved into her chair and let my shoulder touch May's. Lil put her hand out and I eased her into May's lap, where she stayed only a few seconds before climbing back into mine. She tucked herself into my chest, and I pressed my shoulder against my wife. For the rest of the service I felt her sobs.

She didn't look at us until it was done, when she managed a tiny smile for Lil. She took her hand, and we walked from the beach to our car with the other mourners, the minister and Julie and Carl in the lead, then their parents, then the rest of us in heads-down procession. To the cars, to the cemetery, in the blinding cold and chilling sun—that was how it felt, sensory information muddled—to drop Albert's cremains in a hole. *Cremains.* The minister actually said that when we were gathered at the gravesite.

I saw a crematorium once, in Spokane, Washington. It was in a neighborhood, not a great neighborhood, but an okay one. You could see the wavy exhaust coming out the top of the building. Imagine looking at that every day. After a body is cremated they have to pulverize the bones. I hadn't known that.

So their son's bones were pulverized, and Julie and Carl managed to have sex at least once these past months. But they must have a sense they're walking through the same fire. May feels like she's on her own.

She's left me here at our kitchen table, but invited me to Albert's thing. And I'll see her later because she wants to get Lil. All these increments of encouragement and discouragement. I can't stand them. And then I do.

I get up to stick my head in Lil's doorway, and she and May are on the floor, my wife brushing my daughter's hair. They don't register my presence so I leave them to it.

I'm back in the kitchen when I hear the front door shut, and Lil races in, her hair in a neat braid that won't last, to announce, "Mom says we'll go to the beach later."

Such an indeterminate pronoun, "we."

"And then maybe you can help Grandpa whack down that old tree."

She means cut down a dead branch hanging over the roof at May's parents' house. First relief, then jubilation, then anger, in super-fast succession. Jesus Christ, May: *talk to me*.

She meets us at the beach after lunch, and we sit on the sand with our arms around our knees. Our bodies don't touch, but our body heat does, like we're in each other's atmosphere. Lillian's running around, in and out of the water, on her knees and back up and scooping sand into her pail and dumping it.

"Albert's service?" May says. "It'll be next Saturday."

I nod.

"At the gravesite. People will say a few prayers and maybe we'll have a song and—" She lifts her hands and clasps her knees again. "Then we'll get ice cream."

She turns to me. "Do you want to come?"

"Yes, yes. I do."

"It will be religious."

"I understand."

Lil waves to us and we wave back and watch her take a running leap at a mound of sand.

"How far along is Julie?" I ask.

"Three months."

"Wow."

"She said they planned it, even."

"Good for them."

"I don't believe God took Albert. I don't know if you think I do."

I look at her, but she stares straight ahead.

This could be an opening, or a shutting down. "May, I—I don't know. I guess I did."

"I don't believe that."

"Tell me then. What you do believe."

She looks at me. I hold my breath, and into this space she's opened—I'll choose to believe it's an opening—I say, "I love you."

"I know."

Then she dips her head, and I can't see but I sense her tears. I leave her alone with them for a minute, and I say, "May, tell me." I'm afraid it sounds like *Tell me "I love you,"* a command, but she understands me and says, "I don't think God makes bad things happen, but that he's there when they do. Do you remember what the minister said at the funeral?"

How did she decipher a word of it?

"About how God meets us in our sorrow? And rests with us there?"

It's very pretty, and I can see the appeal.

"That's what I believe. I'd hoped you would hear it and understand, like it might be more convincing from someone else."

"I'm sorry, he was difficult to hear." It sounds so lame, and what I want to say is that I wish she would let me meet her in her sorrow and rest with her there. I would hold her forever.

"May, I am sorry," I say, and she is watching our daughter, and the lake beyond.

The night before Albert's thing May comes over, and we make lasagna. We'd told Lillian about the service. I explained that we would get together with cousin Julie and Carl and everybody to say goodbye to Albert once more, to which she responded, "But we already did that." So May said that it would make Julie and Carl feel not so sad to have the family all come to where Albert was buried and say they love him and thank God for taking care of him now, since it had been one year, and that seemed to make more sense to Lil.

The lasagna is autumnal and sort of festive, and we'll have ice cream after the service tomorrow, and we ate pierogies after Albert's funeral, and is there any starker display of mortality than all this fueling? We are so inefficient and weak.

I wake in the middle of the night and get up to walk past Lillian's room. May's not there. The bathroom is empty, and I open the door to the garage and see her car is still parked. She's not in the kitchen, and when I go by the living room she says, "Jeremy."

I back up and stop. She's in the chair by the far corner window.

"I can't sleep," she says.

"Can I get you anything?"

"No."

I'm in just my underpants. There's only a bit of moon filtered through a big spruce tree, but I feel lit up.

"Can I—" I start to say again. What? Can I get us some wine? Can I rub her feet? Can I hold her?

"Julie's upset with me."

I can't move. I don't want to spook her. "She's upset? Why?"

"I didn't act happy enough when she told me she was pregnant, but I'd been thinking about Albert's anniversary. I was shocked. I started crying."

"Oh May."

"Our moms were there and I pulled it together, but yesterday she told me—she actually said this—that she's been handling Albert's death better than I have and I should see a therapist. Jeremy"—my name again, happy jolt—"do you think I should?"

"Do you want to? Would it help you?"

"How do I know?"

"Our insurance covers it." I say this for two reasons, to tell her she can try it and we'll be out only the co-pay, and to emphasize that the insurance is *ours*, because we're married, like the house is ours and Lillian is ours. It's calculated but not insincere.

"She also said that I'm treating you badly."

There's no correct response to this, and I exhale.

"I'm sorry," she says.

"May—"

"And I'm jealous. That is the truth. I am jealous of Julie, who lost her first child. What is the matter with me?"

There is no wailing when she says this. It is still just her solemn voice from the dark corner. She gets up and comes toward me, and in hopeful confusion I put my hand out. I'm cold and I have to pee, but she seems unfazed that I'm nearly naked.

"I should go to bed." She looks at me, and my hand drifts down. "Jeremy, I'm sorry."

In the morning I feel wrecked. I think May does too. When my eye catches hers, my heart, already skittery from coffee and lack of sleep, goes galloping off. After breakfast I claim a headache and get back in bed.

But I am showered and dressed by 12:30, and helping Lil on with her tights. May comes out of the bathroom in a navy blue dress she knows I love, but I only glance at her in the doorway of our daughter's room.

"Come on, Lil," I say, "don't bunch up your toes."

It's a cold, drizzly day. It rained all morning and could start again. At the cemetery I imagine May's people making their appraisals: we came together; we're holding Lil's hands; we look like a family today. Her parents have been polite and gentle this past year, and they don't look at me anymore so much as peer and squint, like they're looking for something. Who knows what May tells them.

The dopey minister is here, and so is that woman Julie got mixed up with when Albert was in the hospital, the Christian witch doctor. I know it's her. She's got that earth-mother-of-the-universe look: flowy purple dress, salt and pepper braid winding her head, and a gigantic brass cross around her neck. The chain takes a steep dive off her bosom, and the cross thwaps her stomach as she walks toward us—thwap, thwap, thwap.

"May, here you are with your lovely family."

The earth mother takes both of May's hands, and Lil turns to me.

"This must be Lillian."

I hoist Lil up and she regards the woman from her perch on my hip.

"And Jeremy, it's wonderful to meet you."

"Nice to meet you."

"This is Margaret," May says.

Lillian turns in my arms and whispers, "You're a weisenheimer."

"Shh," I say and pat her back.

"I've prayed with Julie and Carl," Margaret says. She looks at me. "I used to be a nun."

"That's interesting." Actually, it kind of is.

Back to May. "They are holding up. But how are you, dear? Should we take a moment?"

May says yes and looks at me and I nod. I can handle her family without her.

Lillian and I make the rounds. She hugs her grandparents, and they peer and squint at me. May's dad shakes my hand and claps my shoulder. Her mom hugs me and says, "Oh Jeremy, I'm so glad you're here. I am so glad."

We say hi to cousins and friends, and I keep an eye on May and Margaret, off under a tree, heads bowed. I also keep an eye on Julie and Carl. Good old Julie, my defender. She's not looking very pregnant yet, but she rests a hand above her belly. They're standing by the gravestone. I feel shy about approaching them, but I do it. Lil gives them hugs, and we all look down. It's hard not to.

Albert Yuan Bartelski, 2006–2016, Beloved Son and Grandson, Nephew, Cousin, and Friend

The minister inserts himself, and Lil and I step away.

"Where's Albert?" she asks.

"Lillian, honey, you know this." I suppress a flare of irritation. "Albert's not here. He died."

She looks around. "I know."

May joins us, and I see the minister and Margaret conferring with Julie and Carl. I wish Dr. Phillips were here, and Albert's oncologists from Grand Rapids.

"Why wasn't Margaret at the funeral?" I ask May.

"She had another funeral. For her aunt."

"You didn't tell me she was a nun."

"Yes I did."

The minister raises his hand, and people stop talking and gather around Julie and Carl. Margaret and the minister stand behind the gravestone, and the rest of us face them.

"Friends," the minister starts. He wears a regular suit and tie and a big white sash over his shoulders. "We are here to remember the life of Albert Yuan Bartelski." He clears his throat. "Let us pray." He clears his throat again. "Our Father," he says, and people chime in.

I look down at Lil. She's studying an insect on her shoe. I take her hand. On the other side of her May has closed her eyes and crossed her arms, and she leans so far forward I'm afraid she'll crash into Carl. But the prayer ends and she stands up straight and takes Lillian's other hand.

Margaret leads us in the twenty-third psalm, the one about the valley of the shadow of death. Then there's a mumbling verse of "What a Friend We Have in Jesus," fifteen or so people, a cappella.

There are more prayers, and I wonder what it would be like to put my arm around my wife, meet her in her sorrow and rest with her there. Everyone would notice.

The minister finishes by holding up his palm. "May the Lord bless you and keep you."

It's like a tiny church service. It's fine. It's what I expected.

Afterward, there's some milling about and hugging and crying, but it's cold and I want a cup of coffee. Lil and I wait for May, who's talking to Julie. Maybe they're making up. Maybe Julie's talking about me.

Margaret startles me while I watch my wife, and in her face I can see what my face must betray because she doesn't say anything at first, just gives me a sad, closed-lipped smile.

"Jeremy," she says.

"Hello."

"I asked May if I might talk to you."

"Okay." My heart starts going.

"I know things have been difficult." She looks at Lillian.

"Lil, go hang out with Grandma for a few minutes." I point her toward May's mom, and she trots over.

I look at Margaret. *Who is this woman?*

"Jeremy, I realize I might be overstepping, but I want to tell you I believe May is trying. We don't know sometimes why we have the emotional responses we do. It can be a real mystery." Her speech sounds rehearsed, and when I don't answer she carries on. "And just like you are a mechanic who diagnoses the problems people have with their cars, I like to think of myself as a mechanic of the human spirit." She throws up her hands. "But before you roll your eyes—"

I'd already started.

"Before you roll your eyes, I'll tell you that sometimes I can't figure it out."

I just keep looking at her.

"I can't explain everything going on with May, but I know she's hurting."

No shit.

"I didn't tell her what I was going to say to you. But I think that part of what's fueling this stand-off in your marriage is that she's so deep in she doesn't know how to stop."

I want to hate Margaret and stalk off, but I am riveted. "It should be easy," I say, but I know it's not true.

"I don't think so."

"What should I do?" I ask this to challenge her and, honestly, to see if she might know.

She shakes her head. "There is no real answer. All I can tell you is that it seems this isn't necessarily the end."

I would like to respond that her hedging is small comfort, but the truth is it is something, so I ask Margaret, this stranger, "Does May want another baby?"

She turns away and puts her hands on her hips, so I explain to her profile, "She said she is jealous of Julie."

Margaret is quiet for countable seconds. I count them and make it to seven before she says, "Children cannot save you," and looks back at me.

"I know." But even if this is not the answer, it might still happen to be true, and implied is that May wants another kid *with me*, right?

"The question is not so simple. Define 'want.'" Margaret is irritated, but I don't care. "I suppose the answer is 'yes and no.' Or 'yes and wait.' Do you understand me?"

It's something I say to Lillian. Do not touch the stove when people are cooking. *Do you understand me?*

We stare at each other.

"Jeremy, my point is not that this is irrelevant, but I advise a great deal of patience."

How many more years of patience, Margaret? I look over her shoulder at May, and Margaret turns around and looks too.

"Thank you," I say.

She turns back to me. After a pause she says, "You're welcome. But I mean it. This is not some easy answer."

"I understand."

She sighs and takes my hands. "I wish you peace."

"Thanks."

She squeezes and lets my hands go and gives me a nod that is almost a bow. Then she turns and walks away and I am left with this hopeful scrap of corroboration, but it is no answer and will not be easy.

I find May's parents and ask them to take Lillian to the ice cream place. I let May drift my way. "Lil's going with your folks," I tell her, and she raises her eyebrows but says okay.

We walk to the car and get in, and she is silent when I veer from the ice cream route and end up at the beach. Since it's the only useful bit of intel I've had in a year, I come right out and ask my wife, "Do you want another kid?"

I don't expect her to answer immediately, but she does. "It's a strange thing to want right now, I realize."

My heart reasserts itself. It is not faster so much as bigger, too big. The lake is huge before us, gray with whitecaps and disappearing on one side into nearby cliffs, and on the other into faraway ones, and in front of us into the horizon. Some people need mountains, some people need prairies, some people need cities, and I need this lake.

"Did Margaret tell you that?" May asks.

"You did, May. Last night. You said you were jealous of Julie."

"That isn't all I meant."

"Tell me."

"And my point was I feel guilty about it, Jeremy."

"But can't you support Julie and also be happy?" I lower my voice. "We could have another baby."

She shakes her head. "Please can we not do this now? People will wonder where we are."

"I want you," I say, and it is a sound like *Help* or *Water*.

May doesn't look at me when she says, "I am jealous of Julie because she has her marriage, and because Carl believes in God. And yes, now she is pregnant again, and I am jealous of that too."

There is only our breath and the waves' soughing, muted by the car. And there is also my heart.

"I want to go," she says. "We're supposed to be having ice cream."

"But tell me why it's so terrible that I don't believe what you believe."

"You know that's not all it is. You're disdainful. I embarrass you."

"No."

"Yes. I really think so."

Now she looks at me, so serious, and it might be that my life is over. I remind myself I have Lillian to keep me from walking into Lake Michigan.

"I am sorry," I say. "I don't know what to do."

She turns away. "What did Margaret tell you?"

"Nothing. Just that I should be patient and this is not—not necessarily the end."

"Hmm," she says. It's not even a word. It could mean anything. "I don't know if it's good or bad that she talked to you."

"How did you and Julie meet her anyway?" I'm grasping, and I can hear the shrill echo of my voice.

May inhales. "I honestly think I explained this. She was a hospital chaplain. Which means she drove here this morning from Grand Rapids."

"That was nice of her." It was, more than two hours each way.

"May," I say, gently, gently. "What do we do?" I look at her, and she is looking out the windshield.

"What do we do?" I whisper it this time.

"Sometimes wanting something is inconvenient, Jeremy. Another baby—" She stops and sighs, and I want to say *I love you*. I want to say *Epic love story*.

This is not (necessarily) the end. Be patient, patient.

I lean toward my wife and touch my mouth to her shoulder, not a kiss. She doesn't flinch, and when I straighten up she sighs again, which could be nothing. It could just be her breathing.

LAST THINGS

The last time Dovid and I had sex, almost nine months ago now, two days before he died (August sun, glare on windshields, cell phone, carelessness, EMTs held up in traffic while their sirens whined impotently, my husband stuck on the expressway with his head partway through the glass), he gave me one of the come-on lines we liked to repeat afterward to make each other laugh. "Oh Sam," he said as he unbuttoned my shirt, "Sam, I need you." While he kissed me in a line from throat to crotch, it was just my name, "Sam, Sam, Sam. Sam. *Sam.*"

It often started this way, with the lovey talk that embarrassed me and turned me on, but after that I couldn't predict how the sex would go. Usually it was good, though once in a while it was boring, or I'd realize halfway through I was tired, or I'd start thinking about errands or TV shows or bills.

But the last time was perfect. This is corny, but I sensed we were communicating, that he could really feel how I loved him. It was straight-up missionary-style intercourse, but none of that gymnastic, tantric business could have made it better.

When it was over, though, Dovid got up, found his jeans, and dug in the pocket. When he crouched like that, I could count his vertebrae. Next to my slender husband I often felt ponderous, but he claimed I had the body of a pin-up girl, praise that nearly let me forgive myself my heavy breasts and extra pounds.

From his wallet Dovid pulled out a bill and stuffed it in the pink satin box that had sat on top of my dresser for almost two years. A gift from my aunt, the box—the most horrifying wedding present ever—came with a photocopied Ann Landers clipping about a woman who put away a dollar each time she and her husband had sex, and when they finally counted the money on their fiftieth anniversary there was enough for a trip to Hawaii. "That's some bad investing," I said when I read it, and Dovid asked, "Who's the whore? You or me?"

Now he bounded back into bed and kissed me. "That earned a twenty."

"Seriously, Dovid? We're trying to be frugal and you put twenty dollars in the sex box?"

"We're saving, Sam, remember."

"It's savings with no interest."

"It's a mitzvah."

"I'm still not sure that's how your people intended that word. Have you ever counted what's in there?"

"No, you can't! You have to wait until your fiftieth anniversary."

"By then we'll be in our eighties." I rolled over and nudged him with my foot so he'd scratch my back.

"That's true," he said, making lazy circles down my spine. "Maybe we should shoot for our thirty-fifth. Where do you want to go?"

Sighing, I said, "France?" I'd never been to France. I'd never been anywhere significant. I still haven't.

"Nah, not France."

"What's your great idea?"

Dovid scratched some more and rolled me back over. He put a hand on my breast. "We can go to France, Sam. It doesn't matter. I just want to be with you."

"Oh swoon! Dovid, I need you," I said and laughed, but he moved his thumb to my lips.

"I mean it. That's all I want."

Oh swoon.

Dovid had declared the sex box his favorite wedding present. On the first Shabbos after our honeymoon we had dinner at his parents' house in Evanston, and his sister, Leslie, asked what we'd gotten as gifts. Dovid winked at me, and I put my hand on his arm. "Honey, don't," I said, and so Leslie asked, "Don't what?"

Dovid described the sex box and the Ann Landers clipping and my well-meaning and thoroughly goyish Aunt Darcy. "She's the sort who reads Ann Landers and takes it seriously," he said. "She might even write in. Look for letters signed 'D. in Rantoul, Illinois.'"

Leslie laughed and I pinched my new husband hard above the knee. "Enough," I whispered.

"Dovid, please stop," said Rebecca, his mother.

"It's a mitzvah, Mom," said Leslie, and she and Dovid laughed again.

"That's what I told Sam!" Dovid put his arm around me.

"I don't think it's funny," Rebecca said.

"I don't either," I protested.

"When you start trying for kids you should put in five dollars each time," Leslie said.

"Ooh, good idea," Dovid told her. "We're going to overflow the box. We'll be able to travel the world."

"*Are you drunk*?" I mouthed to him.

"Dovid, your mother asked you to stop," said Gene, his dad.

"I want a niece or nephew," Leslie said. "So you'd better hurry."

"You know why the sex box is truly the best wedding present?" Dovid held up his wineglass. He sounded a little shrill now, as though he knew he'd started something and couldn't back down.

"Dovid," Rebecca said.

"Because that other stuff, the dishes and towels and everything, that has nothing to do with weddings. But the sex box—there's an acknowledgment of what marriage is all about." He tipped his glass toward no one in particular and drank.

"Dovid, stop it!" Rebecca was half out of her chair, her eyes welling.

"Mom, I'm sorry." He stood up.

They looked at each other a moment, and Rebecca's tears started to fall. "Damn it," she said. "I left dessert in the freezer." She shoved back her chair, and we watched her take three fast steps into the kitchen. Gene exhaled and got up and followed her.

"Shit, Dovid," Leslie whispered when they were gone.

"What just happened?" I asked.

"I'll explain later," Dovid said. He sat down.

"Honey—"

"Sam." He shook his head.

We sat without talking, and Rebecca and Gene came back in, Rebecca holding an ice cream scoop and a quart of vanilla, and Gene following with chocolate sauce and bowls on a tray. "The pie will have to wait until next week," she said, "but we can still have ice cream."

"Mom, I'm sorry," Dovid said again.

"I'm sorry too," Leslie said. "You know how we get."

"I do indeed," Rebecca answered as she scooped.

After we had our ice cream and then tea and awkward chitchat in the living room, Dovid and I could go home. As soon as we shut the car doors, I said, "What the hell was that? Your mother wanted you to stop, I wanted you to stop, and I can't believe you would talk about our sex life in front of your family!"

"The sex *box*, not our sex *life*." He started the car and pulled out of the driveway.

"Don't split hairs. The point is that talking about the sex box embarrasses me, and your parents don't want to hear about it either."

"But it is funny, right?"

"Are you listening? Are we having the same conversation?"

"My mother's reaction wasn't about the sex box. That was about you and me having non-Jewish babies."

"Half-Jewish." I turned in my seat to face him.

"Non-Jewish according to her. Religion is supposed to be matrilineal." I knew he could feel me looking at him, but he stared out the windshield, expressionless.

"What do you want me to do, Dovid, convert?"

"You can't convert."

"Why not? It's allowed." I'd done some furtive reading back in graduate school, when we started dating—*Judaism for Dummies*, that sort of thing—and I knew I was right about this.

"My mother doesn't believe in it."

"So? She doesn't make the rules."

"Something you should understand about Rebecca Isaac, Sam, is that she's not so much Jewish as 'Jewsy.'"

"'Jewsy'? I've never heard of that."

Dovid laughed and glanced at me. "God, I haven't thought about this in a while. 'Jewsy' means ambivalently Jewish. It's not a real word. A roommate I had in college made it up to describe his uncle, who looked like the perfect Hasid but would eat the worst, most unkosher stuff—ham and cheese sandwiches, lobster. The uncle thought no one knew."

"Your mother doesn't seem Jewsy. She seems pretty hard core." I turned off the air conditioning and rolled down the window. It was mid-September, and I wanted to feel the city's persisting heat.

"That's the essence of being Jewsy, hard-coreness applied arbitrarily. Like her attitude about conversion. Or the way you have to say some prayers in Hebrew but some are okay to say in English, and there's no pattern to it."

"Or how Shabbos must start precisely on time, but she doesn't care how we get home?" I motioned to the steering wheel. You're not supposed to drive after sundown on Friday.

"Very nice. Exactly." He took his hand off the wheel and placed it on my knee.

I looked out the window and was quiet, lulled by the lights of the expressway while Dovid's hand crept up my thigh.

"You know what, honey?" I said after several minutes. "I think you're Jewsy."

He let go of my leg. "What do you mean?" His face didn't change.

"You never say 'congratulations' or 'good job,' you always say 'mazel tov.' And if we have chicken and rice for dinner, it can't be the cheesy rice."

"That stuff's habit. It's arbitrary, I admit that, but it's not hard core. I'm not insistent about those things."

"You were pretty insistent about the rice the other day."

"What is this, Sam?" He glanced at me again. "What do you care how Jewish I am?"

"I'm sorry," I said, though I wasn't. I was still pissed. "I don't know what I was saying. I mean, gosh, it's so obvious what a great big Jew you are. You're crazy Jewish, Dovid. You're super-duper Jewish. No kidding."

I watched him clench and unclench his jaw. "All right, Shabbos with my family stresses us both out, but I'm serious. What do you care how Jewish I am?"

"Yes, Shabbos stresses us out. Do you have any idea why it stressed me out this evening?"

He worked his jaw for another silent minute. "I'm sorry. I should have stopped when you asked me to. That wasn't fair."

"No, it wasn't."

"I went overboard. But answer my question. Please."

I didn't care at all how Jewish Dovid was, but I considered how I might lie. "I feel insecure sometimes about not being Jewish. You've got such a rich heritage, and I'm not part of it."

I expected him to say something like, "Oh Sam, we'll make our own heritage, and it will be part you and part me, and part Jewish and part not, but it will be ours because I love you and I'm going to love you forever, no matter what my mother thinks."

Instead he said, "I can see that."

"You can?"

"Sure. When I started college my mother gave me this speech about intermarriage, how Judaism gets diluted every time a Jew marries a non-Jew, especially when a Jewish man marries a non-Jewish woman."

"I'm a shiksa."

"Ouch." Dovid looked at me, then turned his eyes back to the road. "I hate that word. Anyway, I didn't like the way she said 'intermarriage.' I thought it sounded prejudiced. But I have to admit she's right. Some high percentage of Jews marry non-Jews, and their children marry non-Jews and so on, and meanwhile the Jewish population gets smaller and smaller. It's a slow devastation."

I didn't say anything.

"But what can you do?" he continued. "People fall in love with who they fall in love with, and what would it really have accomplished if I'd held out for a Jewish woman?"

"Held out? What did you do by marrying me, Dovid? Settle?"

"No, of course not. That's not what I mean." He reached out to touch my hair, and gripped the wheel again. "But it is complicated, and I do feel ambivalent. A lot of us Jews do. That's how we get Jewsy. For the record, though, I'm not truly Jewsy. I'm not hard core."

"What are you?"

He inhaled. "A plain-old American Jew, guiltily apathetic."

We were quiet, and then he said, "I love you. I'm sorry this all came out the way it did." He looked at me, and he did seem sorry.

"Why didn't you tell me before?"

He shrugged. "It's hard to articulate."

"You were pretty articulate just now."

"I mean it's hard to say. To you. And with that crazy Shabbos dinner and you telling me I'm such a big Jew." He put his hand back on my thigh. We smiled at each other. "It came out."

"You've been thinking about this a lot?"

"Sam, I love you."

We were almost home. After he pulled up and parked in front of our building, Dovid opened my door, and he held my hand as we walked up the stairs. When we got inside he seduced me—make-up sex, compulsory. I was distracted, though, wondering whether by this very act we were helping to devastate the Jews. The sex box must have seemed to his mother like a flippant record of destruction, thousands of dollars worth of attempted devastation and a cultural dead end in her line.

After Rebecca stomped away from that post-honeymoon Shabbos dinner, the sex box for me became linked to her. Dovid often skipped the contribution; whether he made it depended on what was in his wallet or if he fell asleep afterward. I'd even seen him take cash out when we were low, and he could never decide whether any fooling-around short of intercourse counted.

But when he did put the money in, there was Rebecca, invading my marriage with her Jewsiness. I wish I'd thrown the box away right after our wedding. If I had, my memory of the last time Dovid and I made love wouldn't have been tainted.

But this is what happens when your husband dies: certain memories bother you more than they could have when he was alive. While you still have him, you can forget what perturbs you and move on, make new memories, but after he's dead he gets encapsulated and you have no choice but to look at what he's left you.

I tried to make up for the intrusion of Rebecca into the last-sex memory by recalling other last things. Time he said "I love you": the day he died, on the phone before he left the office. Meal together: leftover chicken and rice, cold. Outfit: khakis, a white shirt, and a navy tie. Errand: to the drugstore to get contact-lens solution. Book: he was halfway through a third rereading of *Great Expectations*. Movie: *Saving Private Ryan*, his first time, my second; this was also his last cry.

At first I would pace the apartment while I made my recollections, the aimless movement essential for clear thinking, it seemed. This was part of a phase when strange objects and circumstances held the promise of comfort. A cup of coffee on a rainy afternoon, I'd think. God, if it would rain I could drink coffee and find some relief. Or I'd want to sleep in funny places, the roof of my building or a bench in the garden of the elementary school down the street. I craved flocks of migrating birds, cats in windows, solo trips to the art institute. Random, all of it, but consoling too, not the things themselves, but the pursuit, the notion I could go looking for solace and find it.

So I paced around my apartment in a kind of hot pursuit. I'd pause at the windows, and this regular slowing lent rhythm to my walk: bathroom, bedroom, bedroom, bedroom, living room, living room, kitchen. Seven windows. I'd never counted them before.

After about a week of this, I found myself lingering in the kitchen to stare at the L tracks below my building, and eventually I abandoned pacing for the trains, their apparent forward motion more satisfying than my own circling kind. When the man from the rental agency showed us this place, he took us through the other rooms first, had us admire the wood floors and crown molding, the bay window in the living room, the water pressure in the bath, before trying to zip us through the kitchen. But as he'd done in the other rooms, Dovid pulled up the blind on the one little window. "Sam, come look," he said. I joined him, and we gazed at empty tracks so close we might have leapt onto a passing train. The view was pure urban apocalypse, filthy and desolate. I was about to ask if this was a dead line when a rumbling started to our left.

The rental man motioned us back to the living room so we could hear one another. "A two-bedroom in the city for this price," he said, shrugging and holding out his hands.

Dovid put up with the trains for the square footage, but he wore earplugs while he cooked and kept the blind drawn. I kind of liked the central-city feeling the trains provided, the continual reminder of action and pursuit. I could never really claim those trains, though; Dovid mostly drove to work, and I took a different line.

For the purposes of ruminating, the window was too high and too small. I couldn't see out of it sitting down, and standing on the tile floor for very long made my knees ache. If I got about two and a half feet off the ground, I determined, I could sit and watch the trains for as long as I liked.

Making four even stacks of books took a while, but finally I had a fairly stable structure on which to rest a kitchen chair. I was fine as long as I shifted my weight slowly and leaned on the sill to get down. That first evening I sat for two hours, thinking of last things. Kiss: the morning of the day he died, on the forehead because I was brushing my teeth. Cup of coffee: that same morning, cold and sitting on the table inside the front door when I got home in the afternoon. Favor: the day before, when he made my lunch for work because I was tired and crabby.

I sat and thought and cried, letting the trains thrum through the center of me like a bass drum. It was an odd angle from where I perched, precarious and riveted. I could see shapes in the windows like laps and forearms but nothing identifying, no faces, no heads.

Although my purpose for collecting last things was to exorcise Rebecca from my memories of Dovid, I started to wonder about the last Shabbos dinner. We'd missed several weeks, and before that, except for a few standouts like the sex-box Shabbos, Friday nights were a haze of veiled insults and Rebecca's icy tolerance of me.

There was the time Dovid whispered the translation of the Hebrew in the opening prayer—this was early on, maybe the first time?—and Rebecca actually stopped praying. She blinked at us a few seconds before she was able to collect herself and finish. Or when I was asked to be part of the ritual hand-washing—this was several Shabboses in, when Rebecca figured I wasn't going away, I guess—and I butchered the blessing each person is supposed to say. Dovid fed it to me, but Rebecca sighed, then only semi-successfully disguised the sigh with a cough. Or the time Dovid and I had to come separately, I forget why, and I showed up late, with flowers as a peace offering, and Rebecca informed me they could not be removed from their cellophane and trimmed and placed in water on Shabbos. Or the time I sneezed during Kiddush, twice, and Rebecca looked at me as though I'd done it on purpose. Or the time, or the time, or the time.

There'd been this blissful period in grad school when our families did not exist. (Dovid started his second year of the MSW at UI Chicago as I started my first; we met within weeks.) I knew his family was up in Evanston; he knew mine was a several-hours drive downstate, but there was no Shabbos dinner with the Isaacs then, barely any acknowledgment of the Sawyers, my parents, who still don't understand why their only child would run away to the big city and sign up for even more college and marry a Jew and stay after she'd lost him.

After a while my train-perch stewing did unearth the last Shabbos. It was nothing special: mid-July, no air conditioning, vegetable ragout, icemaker broken, mosquitoes, hiccups during dinner, too much wine, strained politeness, relief when it was time to go. That's all, the usual. I don't know why I thought it might have been profound.

A few weeks after Dovid's funeral, which Leslie mostly planned with the help of a couple of their cousins and consultation from Gene and Rebecca—I could barely put two words together or remember to shower; I was in no state to make phone calls and decisions—Rebecca invited me to brunch that next Sunday. I put her off, and she called every Friday morning for six or eight weeks until I agreed. After that, for a few months, we hardly ever missed a Sunday. She would come into the city and take me somewhere different each time, and she never let me pay.

Rebecca of the Sunday brunch was a lot easier to take than she of the Shabbos dinner. We talked about Dovid. She told me stories about him as a child and a teenager and a young man, how he had his own patch of "garden" in the backyard where he possessively tended his dandelions and clover, how he hated sports and cried because Gene made him try soccer in seventh grade, how he was runner-up to the prom king his senior year of high school, how he lobbied for a kosher meal option in college. I kept going to brunch because of the Dovid stories, and I think she kept coming so she could tell them.

After several months Rebecca brought me a photo of eight-year-old Dovid dressed as Superman and a note she said he'd sent her and Gene after he announced we were engaged. "I found this in the back of my nightstand," she told me, "and then I hunted out the picture."

Inside the envelope was a generic thank-you note, the kind you buy in boxes of eight, but Dovid had crossed out "Thank You" on the front and written "Hooray!" I opened it.

Dear Mom and Dad,

I was sitting in my windowless office the other day, bored after umpteen hours of paperwork, and I started thinking how as a kid what I wanted to be when I grew up was Superman (<u>not</u> a social worker with the Chicago Department of Human Services).

I was old enough—seven? eight?—to know Superman wasn't real, but I think I still believed if I tried hard enough I could <u>make</u> him real, I could <u>become</u> him. And then I started thinking about Sam, Salmon, a woman with a name as strange as mine. (Not Samantha? people ask her. Not David? they ask me.)

As a kid, you don't really know what to wish for. You have funny ideas about what will make you happy as a grown-up. If I could go back and talk to my kid self I'd tell him to forget Superman. I'd tell him the thing that was going to make him the happiest, the thing that would truly make him feel like he could leap tall buildings in a single bound, was falling in love. I'd tell him to be on the lookout for a girl with the name of a fish.

Or maybe I wouldn't tell him. Maybe I'd just let him be surprised.

Dovid

Oh my love.

I closed the card so my tears wouldn't smear the ink. "Can I have this?" It came out a whisper. I cleared my throat. "Can I have this?"

"Of course. And the photo." Rebecca waved the waiter over then and asked for more bread. I dried my eyes on my napkin, and that was it. She told me about the time three-year-old Dovid wet his pants in a restaurant and called the waiter over himself, hollering across the dining room, "We need some more napkins, please!" I'd heard that story before, but I didn't stop her.

I wonder how she and Gene read the note when they received it, if it softened them any, or just made them madder. Either way, I had to admit it was generous of her to give it to me. She didn't have to do that.

All that next week I thought about what of Dovid's I could give Rebecca, a note or a photo, or some other knick-knack she'd recognize. I considered his dog-eared and underlined copy of *Great Expectations*, which Leslie had autographed, "Your friend, Chuck Dickens." I considered favorite T-shirts, an award he'd gotten at work, the clown lamp he'd had as a kid.

Evaluating the items in my apartment made me think about whether I was ready to get rid of more of Dovid's things. This was February. He'd been dead six months, and his pants and jackets were gone from our closet, but lots of clothes stayed folded in his dresser drawers. His toothbrush I'd tossed, but his razor and comb and eyedrops still cluttered the medicine cabinet.

And the sex box still sat on top of my dresser. Since he died, I'd tried to ignore it, but now I felt compelled to throw it away. I don't want to make a big deal out of this, I told myself, but when I picked up the box and opened it I cried. I counted the money: forty-six dollars, including the twenty he'd put in after the last time. I reminded myself that didn't mean we'd had sex only forty-six times since our wedding.

It was forty-six dollars I could use. Our savings and my paychecks weren't going very far. I put the money in my wallet and deposited the box in the kitchen trash.

After dark, I climbed up on my perch and watched the trains and cried some more. I held Dovid's note, but I was thinking how the apartment was mine alone. I could sit in this window he hated, and I could throw away the sex box he loved. It felt disloyal, but I don't think the living have any choice but to be disloyal to the dead. Even so, before I went to bed I took the box out of the wastebasket, brushed off the wet coffee grounds stuck to one corner, and hid it in Dovid's top dresser drawer with his socks.

I couldn't bring myself to throw away the socks or anything else yet, though for Rebecca I settled on a framed photo of Dovid and me on our honeymoon at Pictured Rocks. It was a place they'd taken family vacations when he and Leslie were little, and I thought his mother would appreciate seeing him there as an adult.

It was the wrong thing. Better the book or the lamp. But Rebecca smiled and thanked me and put it in her purse. Then she made a painstaking procedure out of zipping the purse back up and hanging it on her chair and arranging it so she wouldn't bump it with her arm, and though she bent her head I could see she was flushed. She didn't want a photo of me, and she was struggling not to show it.

"Pictured Rocks," I said.

"Right."

I turned from her, and I didn't know what to attend to first, the realization she didn't want a photo of me or my colossal stupidity in thinking she would.

Before I could decide, I turned back and caught her eye, and she looked away and said, "For a while, I hoped you were pregnant."

I felt something give way inside and I inhaled and sat up straight, as if to stop this internal toppling. I stared at Rebecca's profile and followed her gaze to a couple standing near the door of the restaurant. The woman was blond and curvy, and the man was tall with dark hair. But besides that, they didn't look like Dovid and me. And the woman didn't look pregnant.

"I mean after Dovid died I hoped that," Rebecca said. "I hoped you'd gotten pregnant right before." She faced me again. "But look at you. Look at how thin. Salmon, sometimes I still can't believe it."

"I can't believe it either."

The waitress showed up and we ordered coffee and remembered to open our menus, and there was all of brunch yet.

"I hope you're not offended by my telling you that," Rebecca said when the waitress left.

I shook my head. I'd hoped it too, but it was a tiny hope, and one that surprised me. When I got my period the first time after Dovid's death I thought, Well, that's over too. First period, last chance: another last thing. But I knew I didn't want a baby so much as I would have liked to keep something of Dovid.

"I've watched you week after week," Rebecca said, "and you've only gotten thinner. Of course, you look beautiful."

I doubted that, but it's true I was thinner. Rebecca was too.

Then our waitress was back, and as we ordered, I thought of how Dovid loved my not-so-thin pin-up girl body, how he probably would have loved me pregnant too, and I started to cry. The waitress gaped at me. Rebecca shooed her away.

"I'm sorry," Rebecca said. "I'm sorry."

"Tell me a story."

She told me the one about Dovid and Leslie getting lost at Disney World, and the one about Dovid winning the class-treasurer election in eighth grade, and I tried to stop crying. I'd cried so many times over brunch. I'd cried because Dovid was dead—he was still dead. Now I cried because Rebecca didn't want a photo of me, and because only when my husband was dead did she wish for a grandchild, non-Jewish though it would have been.

Our food came, and I had to sit there, all through the eating of it. Rebecca kept telling stories, and I kept trying not to cry.

Finally, she took a deep breath and said, "Gene and Leslie and I want to invite you to Shabbos next week."

How could I decline? She didn't want me there, Gene and Leslie probably didn't want me there, and I didn't want to be there either.

"Thank you, Rebecca, I'd love to. That's very thoughtful," I said.

"Oh good," she replied. "We'll see you Friday."

We cut brunch short that day, no dessert or extra cup of coffee, no more stories about Dovid.

There were five days until Shabbos. I thought about what Rebecca might be doing, if she were making special preparations to protect her traditions from my bumbling goyitude. I wondered if she and Gene and even Leslie had agreed on ways they could dumb Shabbos down, reminding one another, "It's just one more dinner," and hoping I wouldn't think I had an open invitation.

I feared I was walking into an elaborate kiss-off, a *last* last Shabbos. Rebecca had put in her time with me, she'd told the Dovid stories, she'd given me the Superman note. She had performed one long mitzvah, and if Shabbos were the culmination of that, I didn't want to participate.

Why invite me now? Because she'd told all the stories she wanted to tell? Because I clearly wasn't pregnant? It felt like she had some secret timeline in mind and that my usefulness to her had run its course.

That Sunday night, when I'd already fumed for hours after brunch, I got up on my train perch. I wanted to calm down, but the longer I sat and thought, the angrier I became. What was so terrible about having a photo with your daughter-in-law in it? And how dare Rebecca say she wished I'd gotten pregnant? Once again, she had invaded Dovid's and my sex life, where she'd never, never had a right to be.

The trains thundered past below, rattling the window and buzzing in my chest—all that speed and metal flashing by, all that pursuit—and I thought of the sex box in Dovid's sock drawer, coffee-stained and empty.

I leaned on the sill and eased myself off my perch. Rebecca was using me to pursue some kind of closure, I was sure of it, and I could use her too. The photo was the wrong gift, so how about this ridiculous wedding present Dovid had loved and through which Rebecca had tormented me for years?

When I opened the drawer, the sex box loomed, luridly pink and satiny from the white nest of Dovid's socks, and I knew I couldn't send it to Rebecca. I was ashamed of the meanness of what I'd imagined, mailing it so she would get it before Shabbos and have time to realize what it was before I showed up for dinner. But I was frustrated too, with my incapacity for revenge, or any satisfying dramatic gesture, and in my frustration I yanked the drawer out onto the floor.

It thumped, wood against wood, and I picked the sex box up and turned back to the kitchen with it. I climbed up on my perch again to unlatch the window, which I heaved open with one hand. The rush of wind in my face forced my eyes and mouth shut, and with the other hand I hurled the sex box at the passing train, at its rumbling and squealing, its mass and latent violence.

Monday morning I was chagrined—there'd been a dramatic gesture after all—but relieved, too. I avoided looking out the window for fear I'd see the sex box lying there, pink in the snow of the embankment, pitifully short of its target.

What I was left with, after the shock and sorrow and fury of that Sunday, was a weekday strangeness, a numb acknowledgment of the inevitability of Shabbos dinner. So when Rebecca called me Thursday morning and said, "Salmon, I need to cancel," at first I didn't know what she meant.

"Hello?" I said. "Rebecca?"

"I'm sorry."

"For what?"

"Salmon, I can't—well, Shabbos."

I pictured her before I understood her: a small, aging woman, thin bordering on brittle, with her hand on her brow, crying.

"Are you crying?" I asked. "Are you all right?"

"There are things I wish I hadn't said to you. I imagine I upset us both."

"Oh," I responded. "Well."

"It can't do any good, and I don't know what I was after." She paused, and then she said, "So no Shabbos dinner, all right? This must seem rude to you. It is rude. I'm sorry."

"Okay," I said. "Okay, I. . . after all of that I thought—"

"I'm sorry," she said again, and now it was a sort of customer-service *I'm sorry*, polite but indifferent.

We were quiet a moment, and I felt myself go hot inside my clothes. "This is hard for me," I told her, and it seemed I'd admitted something important.

"I know," she answered, in the same indifferent voice. "It's hard for me too."

"No, Rebecca," I started, "you still have Gene, and Leslie—"

"Salmon, Dovid was my son."

There was only one response, but it was so obvious I couldn't say it. I almost thought Rebecca would say it, or that she should, but she just said, "I'm sorry" once more and "Goodbye, Salmon" before she hung up.

So I said it to myself, out loud and still holding the phone, "Dovid was *my husband*."

That was the obvious response, but it felt beside the point. So I said, silently this time, And Rebecca, I'm your daughter-in-law.

My husband died in August and now it's May. If I'd been pregnant when he was killed I'd have a new baby, which means I'd have some in-laws too. But I never wanted a baby, and I'd achieved a weird kind of closure with Rebecca, though I don't think you're supposed to have closure with your in-laws. You're still related (aren't you?) even if the one relating you is dead.

Rebecca and Gene mailed me a birthday card in April, and they send checks periodically. The envelopes arrive with those yellow change-of-address stickers on them. I moved out of that two-bedroom apartment I couldn't afford, into a studio whose windows look onto the street.

I don't know if I'll see my mother-in-law again. I might. I could easily run into her someplace. If I saw her I think it would feel like a kind of first, the first time after what had seemed like the last time.

But Chicagoland is huge. It would take little effort to avoid all our brunch restaurants, and every store or park or theatre or street corner I can remember her ever mentioning. Or—and maybe I like this best—I could relocate, probably someplace smaller this time and therefore cheaper (Omaha? Asheville?).

I wouldn't tell her. I would cleanly snip all the threads of my life here, letting go my job, my apartment, many of my things—and Dovid's. Maybe she would call sometime, but I doubt it, because I can't imagine anything else she might have to tell me. And I don't know at all anymore, if I ever did, what she would want me to say.

NOT DEAD YET

It had been ten years of coincidences, and now here was the worst: Dean's second wife had the same kind of cancer his first wife had died from. It was a very common cancer, but still.

They had met in a support group, two surviving black spouses of white spouses dead from cancer. Dean tried to play down the coincidence of the group. Seventy percent of the reason anyone was there was to meet someone new.

They had also both gone to (separate) high school(s) in Philadelphia and taken circuitous life paths (entirely different in timing and stops) to land in Michigan. They both had a shellfish allergy. They had read *Anna Karenina* and *War and Peace* all the way through. Their hair, pre-graying, had been reddish. They each had two grown daughters.

"We both wear glasses!" Dean would interrupt, when this tiresome listing got started, usually by one of the daughters. "We both like peanut butter. We each have two legs. Our thumbs are opposable. Who cares! Not everything is interesting."

His first wife's name was Marie, and a stranger at a party once said to him, "Oh! I have a friend named Mary."

"Yes," he'd responded. "Everyone does." He didn't say, Her name is *Marie.*

If he had a life's motto, this would be it: Not everything is interesting.

Dean detected a bit of jostling over who, primarily, this new diagnosis was happening to. They all had grief cred. His own daughters hung back some, which was decent and fair, but they would have to witness their father's grief a second time. His stepdaughters were about to be orphaned. They were forty-something, self-sufficient. They had their own children. Dean wasn't sure whether having acquired a stepfather as adults would mitigate the finality of orphanhood. Most likely not. They didn't need him. They needed their mother. They needed their own father.

Of course, the one this was really happening to was his wife.

It was happening to him too, though. He didn't want to compete with her, or with any of the daughters. But it was happening to him again, goddammit. Twice he had sat in a doctor's office with a woman he loved to hear a too-young white oncologist foretell her end. This second time his initial response had been quite eloquent, he thought: "Fuck," he had said.

The doctor had nodded, and his wife, bless her, actually snickered at his swear. Then they were off on a discussion of time left and how to preserve its quality. That old topic.

Here was another coincidence: each time news of the diagnosis got out someone had sent a card printed with a—what? poem?—called "Cancer Stops at Hope." *Cancer stops at love. It stops at friendship, and at the door to your heart. It stops at faith.* Well, fuck you, because it also stops at death, but not before taking the long way through pain and precipitous weight loss and vomiting. Both times he'd intercepted the mail (such a lucky coincidence) and tossed out this treacly bullshit like the trash it was.

He felt righteous and rigorous and angry. There was some satisfaction in feeling this way, some relief. It was animating. The first time, though, the anger had surprised him. Why anger? What, rationally, was its object?

"Ah, Dad," his older daughter had said, "you spend all your days at least half-indignant anyway. Maybe just go with it. Be pissed off."

That was up there with the most tender things anyone had ever said to him.

He took long walks, then and now, striding, marching, thumping walks. He winded himself and got his heart rate up. The first time, a dozen years ago, had been easier. That is, the exercise had been easier when he was sixty than it was now, at seventy-two, not the grief and anticipation.

But he could still feel his own vigor as he strode, his heart keeping up in expectation of, perhaps, another two, even three decades. Would he go back to the cancer-loss support group? He would have to examine his purpose.

She wasn't dead yet, his second wife, Lorraine. (Both his wives had French first names, a coincidence no one had yet remarked upon.) Barring a joint accident, either Dean or Lorraine would have to bury two spouses. They had always acknowledged this. He should be glad to spare her.

The doctor had said two years at most, but they all knew that didn't mean twenty-four good months. It might mean a few normal-seeming months—through Christmas? it was now August—then a tumbling decline, then some bad, terrifying months. Maybe he'd have a massive heart attack in the meantime. This was a tremendously selfish but tantalizing wish.

It was how his father had gone, undetected arterial build-up (smoking, red meat, an aversion to [white] doctors all encouraging whatever tendencies his body had stored from conception). He'd been alone. It had likely taken just minutes. And though the shock had been indescribable for Dean and his mother, there was also some relief that what was done was done.

But he was thankful Lorraine wasn't dead yet. Every day he was glad, every time she looked at him or made a morbid joke. He tried not to say *I love you* more than the usual amount because he feared she would hear *I'm glad you're not dead yet.* He fairly pulsed with his excess *I love you*s and his *not dead yet*s.

A heart attack was better than, say, Alzheimer's, cancer in some ways better than a heart attack, illnesses better than accidents, losing a parent better than losing a child. A few good months were better than none, two happy marriages better than none, four helpful daughters better than none.

There were a couple of other cancer families in their neighborhood. This was no coincidence; it was probably the same or worse everywhere. His colleague Morley from the university was around the corner. Morley's first wife had been gone six or eight years; the second wife was healthy, as far as Dean knew. And there was this Asian kid down the street, dead at nine or ten. For months Lorraine had taken casseroles to his poor parents. They had a new baby now.

So Dean was luckier than the dead kid's family, less lucky than Morley.

"In some ways I feel lucky," Lorraine said to him one night in bed.

He had started to drift. They'd had gentle, elderly sex—one of these times would be the last—and he had settled into sleep with his hand on her thigh. He was quiet a few seconds, rising out of unconsciousness enough to catch the echo of her words.

"What?" he said.

"I'm the lucky one. You know."

"Well," he said. "Yes. I am glad I can spare you."

It was a lie. They both knew it.

"Of course," she said, and then, "If I weren't so selfish I would put your pillow over your face."

Dean waited for her to laugh. When she didn't, he said, "Maybe I should do it."

He heard her inhalation.

"I mean—" What did he mean? He was half asleep.

"Well, don't do it to me yet, darling." Now she laughed.

He thought he'd meant himself.

"Maybe I could still spare you," she went on. "If you don't like the pillow, perhaps you can hope for a massive—"

Heart attack.

"Hemorrhage." She laughed again. He felt her leg under his hand, then felt it slide away as she turned from her back to her side, toward him. She laid her palm on his sternum. "But I'm not dead yet."

We both like peanut butter. We both wear glasses. We've both read Tolstoy. Who cares! But how could he not wish for more of all of it? *We're both still alive. We'd both choose to go first.*

"I hate this," he said.

"Me too."

"What is the point?"

"No point. Wrong question."

"What is the question?" Wordplay now. Sleepy banter.

"Eh. No question, no answer. Just. . ."

"What? Just what?" He wanted to know.

"Life. Nothing."

"Life. Nothing." He tried it with different punctuation. Life: nothing. Too shrill and obvious. He put his hand over hers. If he could, if he believed it, he would tell her there was nothing to fear. But they both had too much terrible knowledge for that. So they held hands and waited for sleep, and tomorrow they would wake up, still two complex organisms, big animals with too-big brains, aware of the pointlessness of everything but willing, or at least not yet unwilling, to attend to it all anyway.

SEEING LEAH

Once a week, George's nephew brought him a hundred dollars and two bottles of wine. George would open a bottle, and they'd have a glass together. The money he would tuck into his wallet while Arthur Junior watched. Arthur Junior was his sister's son.

His sister was a potato after a series of strokes. George lived here because she and her husband bought him in when they bought themselves in. This was where all three would finish out their lives, which was convenient for Arthur Junior. He could visit his mother and plead gently with his father to *stop life support already, for heaven's sake; Dad, please, it's what she wanted,* and then swing by Uncle George's apartment to drop off his allowance and sit for a few moments with a glass of wine. It was generous to let George pour him a glass, as though George had procured it, as though he owned anything that he didn't owe to his sister and her husband.

He had long acknowledged he drank too much, but ah, what

difference could it make? What pleasures were left? Not sex. Not in a long time. Food, occasionally. Sleep. TV. Books, sometimes. Music. A bottle of wine per day, one glass each week down the throat of his nephew.

George's five other bottles he bought himself, out of the hundred dollars. It was a barely seemly amount for a single person. He bought the wine when the bus went to the grocery store Wednesday mornings. Lately he'd craved pot, but he had to make do with his bottle per day plus the odd glass on restaurant outings. No more drugs, no more sex, no more money of his own.

However his sister finally died, it would be ghastly. He didn't know whether by stopping life support they would starve her or choke her, or how long it would take. Surely they would let her down easy; they would wrap her tighter in her shroud of drugs and let her body's whirrings stop, and she would no longer be the thing Arthur Junior argued about—gently, gently—with Arthur Senior. But think of it: starvation, asphyxiation.

If he were asked, George would tell Arthur Senior to stop being foolish. *It's still Leah in there,* Arthur Senior had been saying for weeks, but it didn't even look like Leah anymore. No one wanted life support like this. No one except the rightest right-wingers and now his brother-in-law. George would like to say to him, *Arthur, you have lost your mind; she is gone, let her go.* But he didn't insinuate himself. Who cared what he thought? He was only Leah's penniless brother.

He had been saving, though, twenty or thirty dollars at a time. He had nearly a thousand in a dresser drawer. The hundred per week was for "incidentals," Arthur Junior had told him, like coffee or postage stamps, but they gave him coffee and he didn't have any letters to send, so without trying he'd ended up with extra. His Social Security he understood was put toward his monthly rent and fees, and he didn't know where the hundred each week came from. He had had a bank account, but he might have closed it or signed it over to Arthur Junior.

He should maybe give the extra cash back to his nephew, but he liked to look at it. He touched it every day. Arthur Junior would find it when he died, or someone would steal it first. He wouldn't care then. The cleaning ladies could have it.

Arthur Junior sat in his narrow living room now, glass in hand. George was only nineteen years older than his nephew, which meant they were both old men. The younger old man had just been to see his mother. George had seen her this morning. There was nothing to say about it. Seeing Leah was no benefit to Leah herself anymore. They went for Arthur Senior and for anyone who was watching and for themselves, so they would know they had behaved decently.

"How old are you, Art?" George asked. Arthur Junior liked to be called Art.

"Sixty-eight. Which makes you eighty-seven."

George had a feeling they'd had this conversation recently. "Which makes your mother ninety-three," he chimed in, to show he could do the math, "and your dad ninety-four."

"Yes."

"Will you still visit me when they're both dead?" He didn't mean to say it out loud.

"Yes, I will. I always will, George."

"Will you stay and have dessert? We could all go to the café."

Arthur Junior shook his head. "Dad is sleeping. We have another meeting with the doctor in the morning."

"This is good wine." George always got himself cheap stuff.

Arthur Junior took a sip. "It is good. I bought a whole case. But I can bring you something different next time."

"I like whatever you bring." Imagine, a case of wine. How many bottles was that, twelve all at once? "On second thought, how about some pot?" George laughed and Arthur Junior smiled.

"I'd have no idea where to get pot anymore. God, I haven't thought about pot in years."

They were quiet for a minute, remembering pot.

"You could ask your doctor." Arthur Junior was still joking, but George had considered it. On what grounds could he make the request, though? General oldness? He was, regrettably, fine.

He was the youngest and most robust of the three old people Arthur Junior had to look after, and his upkeep might eat into his nephew's inheritance for years to come. He'd never asked—how could he possibly?—but maybe the peace of mind was worth it for Arthur Junior the way it had been for Leah.

"You'll be doing me a favor, George," she'd said when she and Arthur Senior made their offer. "I won't have to worry about you."

That was worth something. Plus, he would help take care of Arthur Senior, be his friend now and when he snapped out of it and let Leah go and it was just the two very old men.

Oh lovely Leah! Remember how lovely? Remember, Arthur Junior, your mother when she was a person and not just an organism?

Arthur Junior was looking out the window and holding his glass. He still had a couple of swallows. He might be thinking about his mother, or he might be thinking about nothing, and George liked to believe he provided his nephew some respite: a glass of wine, a meandering conversation, a window onto the dusk.

In another building a robot breathed for the thing called Leah and a separate robot nourished her, and down the hall Arthur Senior slept, presumably, and would wake back up into the anguish, but for now George and Arthur Junior drank wine and comforted each other.

"Listen, George." Arthur Junior turned from the window and downed the rest of his glass. "Dad said to tell you to go on with the students, but he can't do it anymore."

George nodded. Leah's early prognosis had been hopeful, so Arthur Senior had carried on with his activities. By now, though, they had mostly dropped off.

"Do you need me to talk to someone?" Arthur Junior asked.

"No. I can explain."

"I think there are just a few sessions left?"

George nodded again. The students were a group of about thirty from the community college. Each was paired with a willing old person, and once a week they shared their stories and talked about the news of the day or recollections of historic events.

There had also been an art project. George's student, Lexie, took black-and-white photographs of their hands, his and hers and Arthur Senior's and Arthur Senior's student's. Arthur Senior's student was named Paul. Lexie was very proud of the photos and made a gift to each of her subjects of the "best" one. George's copy was in a cheap black frame on top of the TV, four disembodied hands, two groping for the grave.

"All right, George, shall I wash the glasses?"

George tipped his back and handed it to his nephew. He owned two wineglasses. If he broke one Arthur Junior would bring him a replacement. He also had two coffee cups. Might as well not have all kinds of things to put in the sink together and break in one go.

When Arthur Junior had washed and dried and put the glasses away (George would get one out again; they both knew it), he lifted his coat from the hook by the door and held out his hand, as bony as George's own.

They shook, George thinking how this was Monday, tomorrow

the students would come, and Wednesday he could go to the store with a busload of other old people and get more wine. Wednesday was April 4. Leah would die in springtime.

Lexie and Paul looked so mournful when he told them about his sister. Could they leave a note for Arthur (Senior)? Could they make him a card?

Certainly, George said, and Lexie grabbed a marker and a sheet of paper and folded it in half. She and Paul leaned over the card and murmured to each other, part of the general murmur of college students and old people. Lexie wrote some and Paul wrote some, then Lexie took it back and wrote some more and drew something on the front.

She slid the card across the table and lifted one shoulder. "We're sorry, George. I mean, god, it's your sister."

"Thanks for still coming to see us," Paul said.

Arthur Senior had planned to do this project with Leah, but when the semester started in January she had had her first stroke. So George was recruited to share his story and talk about things like World War II and the Korean War and the sixties. The students had learned to ask *Where were you?* but, honestly, he didn't remember a lot of it, except the end of World War II. Where was he when JFK was killed? Malcolm X? MLK? Bobby? Where was he when the wars started? When the wall came down?

Arthur Senior asked them once where they were on 9/11. Well, they were toddlers. They had no searing memories of that day.

Lexie and Paul were friends, and at first George had pegged Paul as gay, but now he figured the boy was just awkward. Paul was mixed race, of some combination whose details George knew he'd been told. He was tall and might be graceful if he could stop fidgeting. His lingering acne partially obscured his handsomeness, but it was there, and eventually, George predicted, Paul would become aware of it too, and that could put a strain on his friendship with Lexie.

Lexie didn't know that the way she looked at Paul betrayed her. She was in love with him, and he would never ever be in love with her. Though George liked Paul just fine, he wondered whether time and confidence might turn out some future Paul he wouldn't like at all.

Lexie was a heavy white girl, hair dyed black and with a silver ring in her lower lip that George could not stop staring at the first week or two but that he'd since gotten used to. She was not beautiful, but she had an arresting poise that made you want to watch her. She was also very sweet, entirely without the world-weary posturing of so many young people, alarming lip ring notwithstanding. The hand photos had turned cloying, but George forgave her.

"People die," he said now, surprising himself. "It happens to everyone." Whatever their assignment was today, George and Lexie and Paul were not doing it.

This project, the pairing of the young people with the old people, was led by an instructor from the college, a middle-aged black woman named Marnie. She started each session with a reading—a poem, a short article—then gave them an assignment. There had been getting-to-know-you exercises to begin, then timelines of life milestones, sprinkled with important moments in history. They'd made collages one week with cut-up magazines, the old people told to illustrate, on one side of a piece of construction paper, stereotypes about young people, and on the other side, the things they had actually learned from young people. The students were told to do the opposite. The point of it all was—well, George couldn't precisely say. Give the old people a positive activity and a chance to feel important. Give the students some material for their American history class. Something like that.

But today they weren't playing along. George counted on Lexie and Paul to remember the instructions and nudge him when he lost track, but neither had yet acknowledged there was anything in particular they ought to be doing.

"Do you think Arthur will be okay?" Paul asked.

"Yes. He has me." George and Arthur Senior's mutual devotion to Leah bound them, and being left by her would bind them further.

They never talked about money. They never had, except once, when Arthur Senior and Leah laid out the proposal that would save her so much worry. Leah had done most of the talking, the only one of the three of them who seemed unembarrassed to admit that without their intervention George was no doubt heading for indigence.

It was an act of staggering generosity. The initial outlay, the "buying in" of a person, was in the six figures, George believed, and there was also a check written on his behalf for a monthly sum he suspected would shock him. That was the way it worked; what all the front-loading purchased was security. If the money ran out, they couldn't get rid of him.

But Leah and Arthur Senior's money wouldn't run out, even for three people, which explained why George was allowed in. The security Leah had been after was not financial but mental: mind and body, they would be settled for life, tended as they needed it and cushioned at each new stage of deterioration, George included.

"I just wish we could do something," Lexie said now.

"I know," George answered. "That's what everyone wishes. But I think Arthur would want us to do our assignment, don't you?"

The assignment was to describe to your partner(s), step by step, something you knew how to do very well. Lexie described how to make baklava; she sketched the sheets of pastry and the bear-shaped honey bottle and the intricate, brain-like walnuts. Paul described how to change a bike tire. George described how to make mint juleps. The purpose was to illustrate that we all have something to teach others.

First, pick the mint leaves. Choose the small, sweet ones. Gather enough so everyone will get a good portion in their drinks. Smell your hands on the trudge back up the lawn and feel nostalgic for all the summers of the world, though in 1945 you're only fourteen.

Then muddle the leaves in the cups. Do you know what that means, muddle? It means mash them to release the flavor, gently now; don't tear them apart. It means do something with your hands so you don't just stare at your beautiful sister and her beautiful friends like the kid brother you are. Look down with a half smile and your hair in your eyes.

Next, add the simple syrup—simple syrup is just sugar and water, but it has to be cooked to thicken—and then the bourbon. Try to find a classy bottle; I mean it, something good. Your sister's friends think it's adorable that you make their drinks, these fancy summer drinks, drinks for the end of war.

Fill up the cups with crushed ice and use a twist of lemon as garnish. Then stick in a few extra leaves and smell them with each sip. They smell like summer.

"It sounds delicious," Lexie said. "Maybe there's a virgin recipe."

"Or he could buy for us!" Paul said and laughed.

Lexie nudged him with her shoulder, as much to touch the boy, George guessed, as to scold him.

"You're not old enough?"

They shook their heads.

"I hope I don't get in trouble." George scratched his forehead and tried to chuckle.

"No, it's a sweet story," Lexie told him, "making mint juleps for your sister." George wasn't sure what he'd said out loud. "I like that word, 'julep.'"

If Arthur Senior were here George wouldn't have mentioned mint juleps or drinks of any kind. He would have told them how to polish silver or choose a ripe watermelon.

To look at Arthur Senior and George, you wouldn't know the difference, two old men shuffling about in their sturdy shoes. But Arthur Senior had made millions, while George had less than nothing. And George was a drinker, a decades-long, committed drinker—though a functional, charming one! Arthur Senior would not teach nineteen-year-olds how to mix drinks, and George, by all appearances, believed it to be essential wisdom. He may as well tell them how to roll a joint, though that they might know.

Alcohol had always been George's favorite, but with his wine rationed the other drugs came swirling back to mind. He'd tried things, serious things, but he liked the light, party ambiance of pot. It was the mint julep of illegal drugs, sweet-smelling and summery, practically benign.

There was nothing to keep him from buying more wine at a go, or bourbon and mint leaves and granulated sugar—had he mentioned that? It had to be granulated. But it sickened him to picture himself, a tottery old man, in line at the store with bottles and bottles on the conveyor. (Five were conspicuous enough; they gave him a box and set it in the child seat of his cart.) Say he could even wield them properly, say he wouldn't smash any. How would it look, week after week? If he did it once, he would do it every time.

The parameters were essential, even as they allowed some indulgence. Arthur Junior knew he supplied wine to a heavy drinker, and he likely suspected the hundred per week went for more. But George was eighty-seven and well-behaved and he didn't drive anymore. His person and his habits were contained, and he would die of something liver-related or he would die of something else.

He didn't want to embarrass Leah and Arthur Senior, though. He didn't want to be the riffraff. So he drank moderately and let Arthur Senior talk him into this project with the students, and he never mentioned drugs or drinking, until today. But pot! Mint juleps! Even sex! All the old sensory excesses jammed his brain sometimes.

"I'll make baklava for next time," Lexie said now.

"I'll help you," Paul said.

"Baklava," George repeated. Sometimes they had snacks.

"And mint lemonade. We'll call it 'juleps.'"

Sweet Lexie would save him from his misstep, then. She would turn it innocent and present it back to him as a story about brotherly devotion, which it was, but it was also a story about drinking. Not even a story—what did he say to these children?—but a well-burnished sense memory lit by the golden-hour glow of summer and wild mint and the giddy reprieve of new peace. Everyone they knew was fresh and beautiful except the boys Leah's age whose bodies lay strewn around the globe, and here was young George learning to please and charm, and learning to be a drunk.

Lexie and Paul turned in their chairs to greet Marnie, the teacher. At least once a session she checked in with each pair, and now she put her hand on George's shoulder.

"I heard about your sister, George. I am so sorry."

"Thank you." How did she know? Being old was like being a

child sometimes. People talked about you, people you barely knew, nurses and teachers. He patted Marnie's hand, and she took it away.

"How are you and Paul and Lexie getting on, without Arthur?"

Oh, fine. I told them about bourbon.

"Good," Paul said. "But we miss Arthur. We made him a card."

"How thoughtful," Marnie said. "They're not too much for you, these two?" She smiled.

"No, no," George replied. "They're very nice young people." That was meaningless. He had to say something more. "It's almost like having grandchildren."

He felt rather than quite saw their reactions, maybe a raised and quickly lowered eyebrow on one, tilted head on another, pursed lips on the third. It wasn't a major overstep, but he was on the brink of seeming pathetic. Heat traveled up his skull.

Lexie saved him again. "You would be a wonderful grandpa," she said, and Paul and Marnie nodded.

"Thank you for stepping in for Arthur," Marnie said, "and I will see you again soon."

"Certainly."

She moved to the next table.

George felt a bit drunk. Old age could be like that. He had nearly always been able to handle his drunkenness by concentrating very hard, but sometimes it got away from him, as old age had this afternoon, more than once.

"We will see you next time, George." That was Lexie.

"Yes. I'm already looking forward to it."

"Don't forget the card."

His hand patted the table for it.

"Please tell Arthur we're thinking of him." Paul now.

They sounded grown up, and looked it, as they stood and leaned toward him. Paul shook his hand. Lexie gave him a one-arm hug. When she straightened she was flushed—embarrassed? pitying?

Maybe this really was, a little bit, what it was like to have grandchildren. Then, unbidden, it occurred to him, *They could buy me pot.*

"All right," he said, interrupting that thought. He blinked several times and gave them a wave. They waved back and turned to join their classmates exiting the activity room. Paul put his arm around Lexie. *Ah, poor Lexie.*

The other old people were stirring, and George looked at Arthur's card. On the front was a drawing of a willow tree. A magic marker was a blunt instrument, but you could tell this artist was skilled. He opened the card.

> *Dear Arthur* [it started, in what was clearly Lexie's neat and twirly hand],
>
> *We miss you but know you must be with your dear wife right now. We are thinking of you, and we wish you peace.*
>
> *Prayers and all good thoughts,*
>
> *Lexie F.*

Then Paul:

> *Arthur—I don't really know what to say. I feel so sad for you, and I will be thinking of you. Thanks for spending time with me this semester, it meant a lot.*
>
> *Paul*

And at the bottom, squeezed in along the edge of the paper, was another line from Lexie: *Don't worry about George. We'll take care of him.*

Oh, shame. That was the word that came to George, not just the feeling but the word too, stark and spelled out: *shame*.

He would find Arthur Senior and give him the card, and he would concentrate very hard and act like he belonged here.

And he would go to see Leah now. *Oh lovely Leah!* George wanted to say it out loud.

Seeing her, he had an urge to cradle his chest. With a glance at Arthur Senior, asleep in a chair, George flattened his palms at the top of his rib cage and squeezed, felt the reassuring give of skin and resistance of bone. He rocked himself like that for a moment, then moved his arms down and crossed them around his middle and leaned forward.

Even aside from the machines surrounding and entering her and the metal bed enclosing her, Leah herself looked not quite human. Horizontal, she seemed smaller. She appeared to be pooling, her body's geometry oozing out of shape.

He hated to look, and he had to look, and he feared the imprint of this image. Who knew how long past her he would live? He could drag it out and out, waste Arthur Junior's inheritance for another decade. Whatever time he had, he didn't want to have to see this—*this*: Leah.

Photographs were some use, but no match for memory, and there was no way to know what would be retained and in what order, or what would soften and what would not. Part of the difficulty of Arthur Senior's refusal to remove the machines was the persistence of this image, unchanged for weeks now, of Leah not dying but suspended. George guessed Arthur Junior felt the same—they just didn't want to look any longer—and he was glad he had his nephew to argue with Arthur Senior.

But somewhere inside her, and somewhere inside his brain, were all the Leahs she'd been—big-sister Leah and getting-married Leah, Leah middle-aged and older and very old, Leah taking care of him, Leah alert and blinking and making decisions, saving him and saving him again.

George leaned back in his chair and studied his brother-in-law, fallen asleep on his superstitious watch. Leah would not get better, but neither would Arthur Senior. And neither would George.

❊ ❊ ❊

Leah had once feared George drowned. She had talked about it for decades.

Summer 1945, the summer the war ended, mint julep summer: fourteen-year-old George was mascot and bartender to his twenty-year-old sister and her girlfriends. When the surviving men began to trickle back from Europe, he knew to feign enthusiasm and even awe, but he preferred the women and was still man of the summer. He held towels and steadied rowboats and offered his arm. He smirked and tossed his blond hair, long for a boy, and refreshed drinks without being asked.

Since before he could remember, he and Leah and their mother had set up house each June in a cabin on the small lake outside of town. It was cheap and rustic and convenient enough for their father to come on weekends. George and Leah swam and fished and tramped through the woods, and at least once a summer they walked all the way around the lake, a day-long journey, heading west from their own cabin.

The lake was a crater, the clusters of cabins all up the hill from the little beaches, and mint grew near the water, so the whole summer long you moved into and out of its scent. Swimming smelled like mint. Hiking smelled like mint. Fishing smelled like mint. Drinking smelled like mint.

What happened that summer before the Japanese surrendered was George's own memory, no doubt a different thing from observable events, but still only his. After the surrender, though, right after, what seemed like memory couldn't have been. It was Leah's telling and re-telling. It was her terror, when George had only gotten drunk and gone swimming and fallen asleep on shore to be wakened by his hysterical sister.

The way his and Leah's lives turned out would, in large measure, have happened anyway, he was certain. There would have been an alternate catalyst, some other clanging moment of recognition, because George had excess loaded inside him, the way that Leah had duty.

It was a Tuesday when the Japanese gave up, brother and sister hot and bored, prickly with each other and with their mother, and all three trying to carve out a bit of cool privacy in late summer. Leah was eager to go back to college, where she was taking a lazy turn through the classics department, but George kept silent and nurtured his ambivalence about ninth grade and a return to the regular company of girls and boys his age. He didn't know how he'd keep up his drinking.

He and Leah had been outside that day in the middle of August, each in an aluminum chair pulled into the lake, ignoring each other, when a neighbor yelled down to them, "War's over! The Japs surrendered!" It had been coming. Even a fourteen-year-old knew.

Their father showed up that night, with a bottle of wine for their mother, but it was just the four of them at a late dinner on the lawn. No party had taken shape, and George could tell Leah was put out and trying not to be—the war was over! The hoped-for, prayed-for thing had happened, but the reaction at their little lake was subdued. They could hear only incidental sounds of celebrating; the water carried laughter and singing and even, George would swear, the clink of glasses. It was a Tuesday that sounded like any Saturday.

"This weekend," he said, "there'll be a party."

Leah lifted her wineglass and winked at him.

After dinner, their parents strolled around to the neighbors', and George made Leah a mint julep with the last of the bourbon. He handed his sister her drink in its silver cup and had his own—a julep with rum—in a coffee mug.

"What have you got there?" she asked. "Naughty baby George."

They sat on the front stoop and looked at the lake and tried to understand what had happened. "I wonder what it's like in Japan right now," she said.

George didn't so much try to imagine Japan as settle into the idea that he couldn't. It was a grave thought. The world was huge. He didn't hate Japan. Maybe he was supposed to. He'd hardly considered Japan before the war.

"You want another one?"

Leah looked in her cup. "Yeah, sure. The world is saved! Pour me a drink!"

When their parents got back, George and Leah were well into their second drinks, George cupping his coffee mug as though there might actually be coffee in it, or warm milk.

He was quiet making subsequent rounds, aware of their parents' shut and silent door. He and Leah went down the hill and sat in the chairs left on the beach. They talked about the war and about nothing in particular until Leah jumped up. "Let's take the rowboat out. I'll row."

"No, I'll row."

They dragged the boat into the water, and Leah got in and sat on its floor against the stern, where they'd removed the second seat to fit more passengers. She stretched out her legs. "One for the road, George?"

He left and came back with two vodka sours, the stronger one concealed in his mug. He handed Leah her drink and set his in the boat, then eased himself onto the seat and clamped his feet on each side of the mug. In this position he pushed them away from the shore and began to row.

The lake was still, the cabins mostly dark, a half-moon bright in the sky of this saved world. He rowed and drifted, rowed and drifted, and in the drift he lifted the mug to his mouth. Leah tipped her head back, and George kept up their aimless progress.

"Leah?" he said. They were in the rough middle of the lake now. "Leah?" Her head tilted forward, and both wrists rested on the gunwales. Her glass had likely dropped yards ago.

They hadn't walked around the lake yet this summer, and George would like to see his sister's face, and their parents' too, as he strolled up from the east for breakfast. He would eat hearty and sleep the rest of the day and help Leah plan a big party for Friday. If he concentrated hard enough he could swim from here to shore; it didn't matter where he landed. He would walk until he reached his family's cabin.

George set the oars on the floor and slipped off his shoes. Swimming off the boat was easy when he didn't have to worry about waking someone or when he wasn't quite so drunk. He shuffled and leaned and finally pitched himself over with a quick series of movements—feet, hips, shoulders, head—that were, he knew, ugly and that set the boat rocking. He surfaced and whipped his hair from his eyes and treaded water until the rocking subsided, his sister asleep through his plunge.

He'd had decades to acknowledge that what he had done was

desert her, drunk, alone, unconscious, and in deep water. But she had the oars and she knew how to row, and how to swim. The water was calm, the boat seaworthy, the likelihood of her tipping or being tossed so remote that for years he could almost tell himself it didn't matter that he'd left her.

She would report that she had dozed, and when she woke he was gone. There was moonlight enough that she could see a little bit, but the lake was opaque, bigger than in the daytime, smooth and sinister.

It seemed to George that he swam and walked a long time. When Leah found him he was several doors east of their place—no indication of where he'd started or how far he'd gone—passed out in a deck chair with a stripe of vomit along his left sleeve, identifiable when he looked in the bathroom mirror later, even after she'd tried to clean him up outside.

The next day, what he could recall of his swim were the drag of his clothes in water and the punching-forward thrash of his arms. Had he been scared?

He remembered jogging on the sand and smelling mint and counting the cabins he passed (though not how many). He remembered a swift roll of nausea and a series of sounds when Leah discovered him: a yelp, a dog's bark from across the water, then his sister's face in his, her whisper and its wind conflated.

But when she woke, drifting in the lake, it was quiet. He could imagine her first click of consciousness, then the effortful but rapid ascent to the realization he was gone—oars at rest, shoes and mug on the bottom of the boat.

"George!" She whisper-yelled it. "George!"

She half rose and fell forward to slap her hands on the boat's floor. Her neck hurt and thirst was on her, worse than pain, but she choked down that first gasping flush of fear to concede she could not—immediately, by herself, and in the dark—find a body in the lake. George had fallen out or gone swimming and by now he had either made it to shore, or he was drowned.

She'd told him all of this, she'd told him or he'd imagined it, how her fear had hardened enough to allow her to sit up in the bow, grasp the oars, and start moving. And how after a few orienting strokes she had turned forty-five degrees and made for their cabin, her brain running on parallel tracks: one terror and the other not hope so much as bracing practicality. She might be abandoning his body, or she might be moving toward him. Dawn was coming and he had to be conjured before daylight, made to stand erect, unhurt and smirking, and no one the wiser.

She couldn't make any noise, it was god-knew-what hour of the morning. Maybe she should, though, maybe she should wake everyone on the lake. It would have been the courageous thing to do, she would say later. But she was afraid of the blame that would fall on her—she'd let her fourteen-year-old brother drink an uncounted number of drinks, and then she lost him because she was drunk too.

When she got to shore, she jumped out and jerked the boat onto the lawn. He wasn't there, at their cabin. She checked inside, making a quick and noiseless tour, then ran back down the hill, cursing herself for wasting whole minutes.

Heading west, she scanned the lawns, and the unmoving water too, as though it might deliver him. What would she tell their parents? She stopped to throw up in the sand, one neat and clarifying heave. George was very drunk, Leah knew, because she was too.

So she went west some distance, for some unmeasurable amount of time, and eventually turned back and went east, to meet him coming. How long and how far she ran were unknowable details, the dark contributing to the tunnel-vision effects of her single task: *save George*. Find her brother, and revive him. Save their family, save all of their lives. Save the peace of the lake and the new peace of this resurrected world.

A party did materialize that weekend, and she pushed herself through it, carried around the same watery drink all night and moved about the knots of her friends, gay-seeming and lovely. Only George knew she was incredulous that she should be standing up straight among them.

Oh, but picture it the instant he was found: sweet deliverance. He did try to picture it, picture himself as she came upon him, his body slack and insensible. This was the best he could offer Leah—the sight of himself not drowned, not choked, whole and not lost. He had succeeded at that all his life.

Over the next couple of weeks, before she went back to college—a relief for them both—Leah told him what had happened to her, the many layers of her terror. He was fourteen; the possibility of his own end was preposterous, and his sister had been his buddy all summer. Now she'd raised herself overnight into adulthood, and he resented it. So he turned secretive, though he sometimes still sipped from his coffee mug in front of her. She couldn't stop him.

It was no great epiphany, but George would come to realize that he and his sister didn't change; they developed. They became themselves. And Leah—oh lovely Leah!—Leah would rescue him forever and ever. And he would let her.

* * *

George set Lexie and Paul's card by Arthur Senior's plate at breakfast. When he'd stopped to see Leah the night before, Arthur Senior hadn't woken, and George felt awkward about the one-sided intimacy of having watched his brother-in-law sleep.

Arthur Senior read the card and looked at George. There were tears in his eyes. He was like this now, one reason George had made no attempt yesterday to let him know he was there. The other was that Arthur Senior could use the rest.

"They say they'll take care of you."

"Yes," George said, before remembering he shouldn't let on he'd read a card not addressed to him.

Arthur Senior sighed. He folded the card and put it in his breast pocket. "Just like Leah."

"Well." Not much like that at all. And hadn't George done some taking care of the students? Wasn't he taking care of Arthur Senior now?

"Shall we go after breakfast?" his brother-in-law asked. He meant go to see Leah.

George nodded. "Will Art come?"

"Later, I think." Arthur Senior paused to take hold of his coffee cup. George watched its tremulous progress from the table to Arthur Senior's mouth. He watched his throat working. Ah mortality, eating and drinking, and then processing waste. He turned away for the cup's clattery return to the table.

"We'll talk to the doctor tomorrow," Arthur Senior went on. "Or maybe it's today."

When Arthur Junior was around, George could stand behind his nephew's disapproval. Arthur Senior would say *It's still Leah in there,* or some such nonsense, and George didn't have to think about his own reaction because Arthur Junior would exhale or run a hand down his face or make a low sound in the back of his throat, and George could remain neutral, sympathetic to all.

But without his nephew, he didn't know how to act. Arthur Senior didn't require anything except commiseration, but George was wary he might forget himself and say something revealing. Something to indicate he still felt some claim to his sister. Something to indicate he thought it was past time to let her go.

They were joined at the breakfast table by a couple of other milky-looking old people, and then a couple more, all participants in the project with the students. They said the expected things to Arthur Senior—*so sorry, we miss you; oh George, you too, so sorry*—and then George and Arthur Senior were folded into a winding conversation that contained nothing of interest but nothing to distress, either.

He let it go on for several minutes. One couple were Phyllis and Stephen, the other he wanted to say were Nancy and Yancey, but that couldn't be right. These people were fine. One expected to sit down to breakfast and have a pleasant conversation, even if someone else's wife or sister were dying. Phyllis and Stephen and Nancy and Yancey knew that one day what was happening to Arthur Senior and George, and to Leah, would happen to them. They would either go first or be left, and the structures of this place would bear them up.

It was time to extricate Arthur Senior, though. He'd had only a cup of coffee and a wedge of pineapple and one piece of toast, but George knew he could not be persuaded to eat more.

"Pardon us," George said.

"Of course," Phyllis answered, and she spoke for all of them. Of course Arthur and George were wrapped up in Leah's dying. Phyllis and Stephen and Nancy and Yancey would want the same leeway to depart the breakfast table ten minutes after others had sat down, when it happened to them.

George stood and nodded, and he cupped Arthur Senior's elbow. Arthur Senior nodded too, and he let George hover while he backed out his chair and gripped its arms to raise himself.

There was another round of polite murmurs, and Arthur Senior held up a hand. "Have a nice breakfast," he said, and it was like a benediction. George could not in any way be said to want to see Leah right now, but he would do it for his brother-in-law.

So they went. They saw her. She was the same, and Arthur Senior was the same, and George was too. He wanted to say something profound, make Arthur Senior understand he would be taken care of and held in compassion, and that whatever happened to Leah in death could not be bad because it had happened to billions of people before her, and animals and insects and plants. No one had asked for any part of it, but shouldn't there be solace in inevitability?

Arthur Senior fell asleep in his usual chair, and George watched him. Soon this would be over, and Arthur Senior would have to find something else to do, but George feared they'd have a hard time distracting him from the ultimate futility of a good night's sleep or a piece of pineapple and some toast.

George had never been to anyone what Leah was to Arthur Senior. He had married twice, forgettably. Both his wives had remarried and had children and were dead now, and he recalled his wedded intervals not with bitterness or regret but with something like the unreality of waking from a bizarre but not especially upsetting dream. Not everyone had a great love. He wished he had the way he wished he'd been able to visit Japan. Alas and oh well. You couldn't experience everything.

George stood. He glanced at Leah and crossed to Arthur Senior to squeeze his hand. The older old man slept on, and George pressed a palm to his cheek, and then—after hesitating, and only briefly—to his heart.

When the students came back it was not Tuesday, as usual. It was Saturday, and George was on time only because Nancy, of Nancy and Yancey, stopped by to remind him.

"It's on the schedule, but I thought—" she dipped her chin and held up her palms "—you might be preoccupied."

"Yes yes, thank you." George rapped his forehead with his knuckles and smiled at her. "It starts when?"

"Ten-thirty."

He looked at his watch. It was ten-fifteen. "Then I will see you in fifteen minutes. Thank you, Nancy."

"Actually, it's Audrey."

"Oh, of course. Audrey." He rapped his forehead again and bowed to her and shut the door.

George went to the bedroom and sat on the edge of the bed. He had been up for hours, neatly dressed and with combed hair and brushed teeth, but he felt unprepared. His heart was going, and damp started in his underarms to bloom across his back and torso. *They could buy me pot.*

The thought had occurred to him just that once, days ago. *Oh, shame.* He looked at the dresser and pictured the money in its top drawer, and he stood, shaky and sweating. He exited the bedroom, and the apartment, and reminded himself to act like he belonged here.

Downstairs, Lexie was leading the set-up of paper cups and plates at a table in the corner. There were gallon jugs on the floor, and she left the room and came back with a large covered baking pan. Paul followed with another one.

George had sat at their usual table, and Paul spotted him. "Baklava," he called. "And mint lemonade."

Lexie set down her pan and turned and waved. She made some instruction to another couple of students, and she and Paul crossed to George.

He stood, and they grinned at him. "I am sure it will be delicious," he said. "What a decadent brunch!"

"Thank you, but please sit, George," Lexie said. He did, and she leaned over to hug him. "Will you take some to Arthur?"

"Yes, certainly. He loved your card."

A mournful shadow crossed both young faces. "How is—" Paul started.

"The same," George said. "She won't get better." They looked at him, stricken. "I am sorry. I don't mean to make you sad."

"It's okay," Lexie said. "Sometimes it's good to talk about it."

"My sister is ninety-three years old. She's lived a long time." *Stop*, George thought.

"Of course," Lexie answered. "But it's still sad."

"It is sad," George agreed.

"Well," Paul said and looked at Lexie.

"We'll be back in just a minute."

George watched them walk away, and Lexie straightened up the snack table while Paul hung around with his hands in his pockets. At some word from her, he said something to Marnie, their teacher, who nodded and stepped to the front of the room.

"Welcome, everybody," she said, and there was a shuffling minute or so as old and young people found their chairs. Paul joined George, but Lexie stood next to Marnie.

"I know we are eager to get started, but first we have a special treat prepared by Ms. Lexie Fotopoulos."

"Baklava and mint lemonade," Lexie said. She smiled at the room, and George watched her eyes slide to Paul.

"Are you Jewish, dear?" called an old lady behind George.

"Um, I'm Greek." Still looking at Paul.

"Oh," the old lady said. "I'm Jewish."

Lexie giggled. "So. . . I just wanted to say thank you to everyone, especially to my new friend George."

George waved, which felt silly, but her acknowledgment seemed to call for some response.

"I think everybody knows his sister is ill." Lexie paused, and the air around her appeared to tremble before George realized she was choked up. He should be touched, but the statement was apropos of nothing.

She pressed her sleeve to her eyes. "Anyway," she went on, and took a breath. "This has been a really great project all semester, and I can't believe it's our last time! So please come have some baklava and lemonade—and Paul helped too."

There was a bit of applause, and George let Paul fetch him his portion. This was their last time, then. Lexie and Paul re-joined him, and George tried to recalibrate his brain. How many more sessions did he think they had? By which he meant, how many more weeks to contemplate their buying him pot, and feel ashamed for it?

"I will miss you," he said. He looked at his three squares of baklava on their paper plate.

They would miss him too, they said, and George asked what they would do for the rest of the semester.

Paul shrugged. "Talk about what we've learned."

"And write a big paper," Lexie added.

"You'll write about me?" George asked.

"Yes, partly," she answered. "Remember?"

George picked up a square of baklava. He didn't care much for honey.

"Do you have any bourbon?" Paul half-whispered.

George looked at the boy. "What?"

"He didn't mean it," Lexie said. George looked at her, and in her face he saw reflected the alarm and confusion that must show on his. "Like, for mint juleps?" she said. "It's a joke."

"Oh yes," he answered, and chuckled. "You'll get me in trouble yet."

The baklava was chewy, and it took some concentrating to get through. But George had all his own teeth, and he chewed and swallowed two squares and had a gulp of lemonade—which was delicious, with the flavor of lemon and the bite of mint—before excusing himself.

He moved as quickly as he could down the hall to the elevator and up to his apartment. His tongue worked at his teeth, and his heart flub-dubbed, but after he'd crossed the threshold and opened the dresser drawer and touched his pile of cash, he slowed down.

He counted out $100. Who knew what it cost these days, but $100 would surely get him at least a quarter. Wouldn't it? That might last a month, if he rationed a bit, and when it was gone, well, he would still have wine. Maybe he'd find he didn't like pot anymore, and this last nostalgic go would satisfy him. Or maybe he could somehow get more.

There were places now where pot was altogether legal. Not here, but even so, there had to be better, more efficient, less awkward ways to get it. George could not guess what they were. He might give the students something extra, a gift. Would that make the whole operation less ignoble, or vastly more?

This was absurd, of course it was. He had nowhere to smoke.

Or maybe he wouldn't even try; he could eat the pot, bake it into Lexie's baklava.

George counted out another $400—students were always poor! it was just a gift!—then folded these bills tightly around the smaller bit of pot money and shoved the neat package deep in his front pocket.

Back downstairs, he entered the room as laughter ebbed. Lexie and Paul explained that everyone had written down the most important thing they'd learned this semester, and now Marnie was reading them aloud and they had to guess who'd said what.

"And that's funny?"

A few were funny, they told him.

"Should I do it?"

They found him some paper and a pen. *I learned*, George wrote. He drew a curvy line under that. *I learned...*

He folded the paper and put it in his pocket, sliding it under the wad of cash. Lexie and Paul made no acknowledgment. It wasn't that he would say he'd learned nothing, not exactly. He'd enjoyed the project, he liked the students, he'd felt appreciated and, indeed, taken care of, but he was lazy and old.

If Arthur Senior were here he'd have something earnest to say. But George didn't have it in him to channel his brother-in-law.

He had behaved oddly this morning—snapping at the jokey mention of bourbon, disappearing for what must have been fifteen minutes, refusing to participate in the day's activity. George touched his cash. He couldn't bring it up. It was too weird and sordid, and if he knew Lexie at all, she would be appalled. She might even cry. Plus, they were going to write about him. He had to shape up. It was only for today.

So he sat up and smiled while the rest of the "important things learned" were read and their authors revealed. When that was done

Marnie read a long poem called "Farewell," which was little more than a list of translations of its title: *au revoir, auf wiedersehn, adiós, arrivederci, sayōnara*. She made a good attempt at pronouncing them all, and when she finally finished Lexie whispered, "I love that." George reached across the table to pat her hand.

It was almost noon, and Marnie was winding up. "I will give you a few minutes to say your goodbyes—your *au revoirs* and *auf wiedersehns*. Thank you, everyone, for working as hard as you did and for being so open-minded and open-hearted. I have enjoyed this partnership very much, and I feel honored to have led you through it."

Paul started the applause. Someone behind them whistled and Marnie bowed, and they all laughed.

"Well," Lexie said, and now she and Paul pointed hesitant smiles at George. Lexie was teary-eyed again, and Paul bumped her shoulder with his. She turned and gave him a look of such longing that George caught his breath.

He was expected to wrap this up and send them on their way, and he would do it. He would not mention pot—though it might very well be simple for them to get it.

That his thinking had gotten this far, that there was $500 in his pocket, as casual as a couple of quarters and a handkerchief, meant he would need to concentrate his hardest to get through the next ten minutes or so. He would imagine he was drunk and concentrate as hard as that.

"I speak for Arthur too, I am sure, when I tell you how rewarding this project has been," George started. He paused and laid his hand upon his chest, Pledge-of-Allegiance style, then removed it and touched his cash before folding his hands in his lap.

They kept smiling. He had made a good beginning. "And so. . . I wish you the best for your studies, and for your promising young lives. For old people like me, it is heartening to see such good sense and concern for the world in the youth of today, and I thank you for spending time with me, and with Arthur, and expanding our horizons." A tentacle of thought reminded him of money, and of pot. Smoking pot or knowing where to find it didn't make them bad kids; it wouldn't have to be pathetic, it could be matter-of-fact.

But who else in this room would entertain such a thought? George grabbed hold of the lingering tentacle and stuffed it down, down.

The students stood, and there was a round of hugs and handshakes. Lexie dashed away and came back with a plate of baklava and a half-full jug of lemonade for Arthur Senior. She hugged George again and was openly crying now. Oh, this girl. She would be irritating if she weren't so sincere.

They told him thank you and gathered the empty pans and jugs and joined the rambling exodus of the young from the old. At the door they turned and waved once more and were gone.

So, he'd done that. His chance past, George stayed seated and tried to stoke his relief at not having mortified the students or humiliated himself. Goodness came easily to people like Arthur Senior, but for George it was exhausting. There was so much vigilance required to manage the rot inside him, build up layers like lead to contain it.

But he wanted pot. He wanted pot as well as wine, and he could contrive some way to smoke it. There was a bit of woods nearby; no one could stop him from taking a walk. And if he were found out, who would call the police on an old white man smoking pot? Though if any shame should fall on Arthur Senior, George would rather die.

He touched the money and made no move, until minutes later, when he did. As he stood he felt woozy, and he leaned against the table. Seconds ticked away, added to the minutes he'd already wasted. He pulled out his roll of bills and clamped his fist around them.

Outside, George sat on the bench at the edge of the portico and scanned the parking lot. He didn't know what he was looking for, a bus or lots of junky student cars. He sat for five or ten minutes, getting cold.

They were gone. He should take his money back inside and have several glasses of wine. He wanted pot—so what? He might also want sex sometimes.

That Lexie and Paul were gone had saved him. His whole life had been like this. Times he'd dodged humiliation or disaster were only lucky. Never arrested, never fired, never out on the street, but drinking always, and profligate too. Smart and charming but with a self-destructive swath as unalterable as shoe size or eye color. Leah knew it, and that was his best bit of luck.

Oh Leah! Here sits your naughty baby George, with a handful of sweaty money and ill-considered plans and the same desires in old age as ever he had.

Leah's strokes had gone from mild to severe and then grave in such heaving stops and starts that there had been no proper time to say goodbye. George was there all the while, hanging behind Arthur Senior and Arthur Junior, when she could still talk to them, and later, when she could only blink or move her mouth a little. But he didn't remember their last words to each other or any significant looks or hand-clasping.

You hoped for peace and acceptance all around, but most dying, George guessed, involved abruptness and confusion and panic. Not that anyone had behaved out of order, but it seemed strange that only now did he register he hadn't said goodbye, and wouldn't. There was a lot of bustle in dying, and in attending the dying.

Oh Leah. He rubbed his forehead with the heel of his empty palm, then transferred the sweaty money into it. He was alone under the portico on this chilly day, and was the only one who would know he held $500 and had considered hitting up college students for pot. He'd only thought about it, though; he hadn't done it.

What happened next George tried very hard to prevent, which would be some comfort when he thought about it later. It was only a few seconds of trying, as his money hand began to prickle like he'd been sitting on it and his vision to narrow by creeping gray increments, before he felt himself pitching sideways. He pitched and pitched to the side and then forward, and his consciousness left him in the middle of his fall.

❊ ❊ ❊

Leah had left the baby with George, and when she got back they were gone. She wouldn't say *worry;* what she felt upon seeing the empty spot where his car had been and then calling an echoey hello into the house was only a pulse of uneasiness. She felt it whenever she left Arthur Junior. In his first few months she had felt it whenever she set him down or handed him off, to gather herself or just rest her arms, which were stronger now but quivered always. She feared they would give out some time. She feared rest was something no longer available to her.

She also felt a separate uneasiness for George. But that she had been living with for years.

They were at the park, perhaps. They were somewhere. Half an hour later, Leah had put her packages away and was studying her to-do list, the uneasiness growing and her arms still quivering but her focus on her tasks.

The phone rang, and she recognized the fluttery inhalation before her husband's sister said, "Leah, it's Dolly. I just drove past the quarry and found George." She inhaled again and held it, as though waiting for the weight of her words to descend. You couldn't be certain of Dolly's motivations when it came to George. The torch she'd carried had been doused by his indifference, and she was too old for him besides. Now, he was rigorously civil to her.

"Is that right," Leah said. So maybe they had gone to the park and were taking the long way back.

But Dolly went on, louder. "He was stopped. Sleeping in his car is what it looked like." She paused, once more marshaling her breath. "I mean, it's 3 p.m., Leah. He was passed out."

"I was just on my way out the door. I will swing by there." Leah knew this response was bizarre, as if by her apparent calm she could make her sister-in-law second-guess what she was reporting. She swallowed once to smooth out her voice. "Thank you, Dolly. We will see you tomorrow."

"I'm closer," Dolly said. "I went by twice to be sure it was him, but I should have stopped. I just hurried home to tell you."

"No. I'm going now." *What about Arthur Junior?*

"Should I call the police? Maybe—"

"No!" Leah exhaled. "Please, Dolly. All right? I am asking you not to do that."

It was a dozen yards from the road to the quarry's edge, past tall guardrails. Leah could name two suicides, plus the car crash that had instigated the guardrails, but the quarry's depth held no more threat than the lake or the railroad tracks. You would have to make some effort to tumble over its cliff.

She pulled up behind George. He was stopped well off the road, well back from the guardrails, a decent parking job though a conspicuous spot for it. Half a dozen cars zipped past.

Leah got out and approached his car. The passenger side faced the quarry, away from the road, and she peered in the window. At the sight of her son she heard her own one-note, mewling animal sound, out before she could stifle it. He was asleep in his little chair, hooked over the front seat. She yanked on the handle, and the door swung wide open to slam back shut. She opened it again and he was blinking at her. After a few seconds he pumped his legs where they dangled from his seat and thrust out his arms, shrieking.

She reached in and plucked him free, taking in George's white throat, his open mouth, his hideous breath as she straightened. Arthur Junior was wet, but she pressed him to her chest. She slammed the door then let her hip fall against it, felt his throbbing heft in her arms.

Cars continued to shoot past, but she turned only at the sound of wheels on gravel, to see a police car inching toward them. Had Dolly called after all, or was its arrival coincidental? She should have shoved George over and driven them all away, not given herself a moment to realize her relief. She could have walked back later for her own car.

The quarry wasn't a picnic spot or a scenic overlook. It was an abandoned rock hole on a busy road. A stopped car was notable, though George's gray Plymouth—and his blond head, tipped back in the driver's seat—might not be recognized except by the likes of Leah, or Dolly, who would be looking for him.

She hadn't really looked at George yet, but it was easy to guess this scene appeared to be almost exactly what it was. The police officer got out of his car and came toward her. When he stopped she saw he looked familiar, and she could probably introduce herself and watch him turn deferential at her name—her husband's family's name—but she said nothing.

"Everything all right, ma'am?" he asked.

"Yes, thank you."

"Is this your car?"

She looked at it. "Yes," she said and met the officer's eyes. She shifted Arthur Junior and he sighed, a whistle through his nose. He pressed his forehead to her shoulder. She could smell the urine soaking him and now seeping through her dress.

The policeman held her gaze a moment. He was young, maybe younger than she was. He walked to the driver's-side window and looked in at George. He rapped twice on the glass.

"Who's this?"

"My brother."

"Was he driving?"

"No."

He looked back at her, a prompt to explain herself, which she would not do. Without considering it, she had chosen a strategy.

Leah didn't know quite what she was risking. She had lied to a police officer, but she was only a young woman with a baby. If George were discovered alone like this: behind the wheel, unrousable, his breath betraying him, he'd be picked up, no doubt. But his sister had happened by and that turned the scene benign. She was here to help him. The officer could move along.

In an hour, say, she would be home, Arthur Junior changed and napping; George installed in his apartment, propped on one side with pillows and sleeping it off; herself in a fresh dress, finishing the prep for Arthur Junior's birthday party tomorrow; and no one the wiser. There was Dolly to consider, but she apparently had not detected the baby in the car when she spied George.

What would actually happen would require three hours, by the time Leah drove George to his place, dragged him inside (she would have to slap and shake him awake), and made certain he could not flop onto his back; then walked the few blocks home to change herself and the baby, who would be full-on wailing; and finally trudged the two miles back to the quarry, pushing a marginally happier Arthur Junior in his stroller—*a nice sunny day!* she would babble at him; *let's take a walk!*—where she would find a parking ticket stuck under a windshield wiper. (Same officer? It wasn't clear.) Then when Arthur Senior got home—*so sorry he'd had to go in on another Saturday, what could he do to help now?*—the baby would finally be asleep, though likely to wake in the middle of the night, and Leah would be in her third outfit of the day, no further along on the to-do list she had left hours ago. But cheerful, cheerful! Revealing nothing.

For now, though, she was saving her brother from arrest.

"Ma'am—" the young officer started.

"I'd like to get my baby home," she said.

"Whose car is that?" He pointed at her own blue Chrysler, behind the cruiser he'd positioned between her and George.

She looked. "Just a car," she said.

Leah felt the quiver building in her arms, and Arthur Junior had started the rapid exhalations that preceded a tantrum. She shifted his weight and shifted it again. She stared at the policeman. She would not look away.

"I need to see your driver's license," he said finally.

Of course he didn't. She tipped her head toward the baby—see? her hands were full—but the officer only blinked at her. "Ma'am," he said.

They studied each other a beat longer. Her license was in her purse, which she'd left on the dashboard, and he was staking something now on this demand. Leah hoisted Arthur Junior and walked to the Chrysler. She didn't hurry. So this was her car. She hadn't said it wasn't.

She opened the passenger door and set the baby on the seat. He huffed and kicked as she leaned over him for her wallet. When she'd pulled out her license, she straightened for only a second, then picked him back up, trying not to think how heavy. A car missing its muffler chugged by, and she tried not to think of drivers gaping at them either.

Leah watched the policeman as she walked the few steps back to him. He had turned toward the road. "Here." She held out her license. Her name would be revealed, then. She hoped he would note she hadn't tried to use it on him.

He took the license, looked at it, glanced at her, looked back down. Around here and for a few adjacent counties, hers was a name like Roosevelt, like Rockefeller. She had married into the local Vanderbilts or Carnegies and taken their name with some ambivalence. Her father-in-law was a real estate broker, residential, commercial, and rural. His full name was everywhere, and for the last couple of years her husband's had been too.

"So now you'll drive this one?" The police officer lifted his chin toward the Plymouth.

She nodded, and he handed back her license.

She crossed to retrieve her purse from her own car, then turned around toward George's. She opened his passenger door, to have someplace to put the baby down again for a moment, and when she did the tantrum began in earnest. Arthur Junior was a year old tomorrow, but Leah had never become inured to how distressing his cries could be. He sounded now as though jolted by physical pain, each outbreath a swift unfurling to a pitch she feared could sink her; more than his ostensible misery, the noise was what would send her under, start her sobbing herself. She couldn't wait until he was old enough to understand he was fine, or at least be told.

She kept one palm on his chest—"Please," she said, "Please"—as she dropped her purse and unhooked his little seat to set it on the floor.

Her brother still sat behind the wheel, and she hated to look at him. She pulled on his arm and he tipped her way, but slumped when she let go. "Jesus, George." She whispered it, though even if she yelled he'd hardly be able to hear her over Arthur Junior, or through his own tanked-up brain. She pulled on him again, dropped his arm, then picked it back up and flung it at him. It landed in his lap like a football or a dead fish.

The police officer appeared at her side. "I'll push," he said. He went around and opened the driver's-side door and moved George to the middle seat, lifting more than pushing. It was done in a few seconds.

Leah motioned toward herself and he nodded. She scooped up the baby with one arm and his chair with the other, and she and the policeman traded places. Neither of them said anything, about how bad George looked and smelled, or about how the baby seat had been in his car.

She stood at the driver's side and watched her brother being lifted again. The policeman straightened and shut the door, and she leaned in to hook the little chair over the middle seat and settle Arthur Junior into it. He screamed, directing his rage at her face. She touched his head, then one knee—*you're fine, please shut up now*—and unbent to look over the top of the car.

"Thank you," she said. When the policeman didn't answer she said it again, louder, "Thank you," and added, "You did a good job."

He stood still for a few seconds, then nodded at her and pivoted. She called after him, "Officer? Can I tell someone for you? Your boss?"

There was a hiccup in his gait, a half-second's hesitation before his foot fell once more and he strode away.

She would say he'd stopped to see if they were okay. Her brother was sick, or her baby was sick, something like that, and he'd helped her. Just a small commendation from a citizen.

A citizen with her name. She had wanted, after her humiliation, to put him in his place a little. She had behaved like a rich lady. There was no chance to attend to this realization now, though she'd like to follow him and apologize. She could tell him her real name and say that maybe they'd gone to school together—he was a few years behind, perhaps, or from a town over?—and confess that her brother was a drunk who had apparently been into her liquor, and then he put his nephew in the car.

She got in now and checked the mirror. The police cruiser was running. She felt for the key and turned it, then crept toward the road. People looked her way as they sped past.

When she pulled out, the police officer was right behind. He followed for a minute or so, long enough to make her think he intended to go wherever she was going, stop to observe but not help anymore while she struggled to unload and buttress George, then tail her home and watch her carry her livid, urine-drenched child into the house.

But he turned right at the first light, where she was stopped waiting to go straight, and she felt anew the quiver in her arms, heightened by a thud of relief.

At the second light, she looked at George. He leaned against the window, his face turned from her, appearing merely to nap. She loved George, and she loved Arthur Junior, but she couldn't help considering how much simpler her life would be if she had grown up an only child and become a childless woman. She had never actually wished for a sibling or a baby. She couldn't recall wishing for a husband either, but Arthur Senior had come along, and him she would choose again and again.

She would not tell him what had happened, though, not right away, maybe only years from now. She would focus first on the birthday party and on their child, for whom the responsibility was partially his. George was hers alone.

Her husband had had a few years to witness his brother-in-law's behavior, to assure Leah he was just feeling his youth and would straighten out. She'd told him about the time she feared fourteen-year-old George drowned, and the two men had chided her for her dramatic imagination. *Poor Leah, but George was fine the whole time!* Arthur had a few drinking stories of his own, and so did she. Leah had laughed with them, but it was different for George. She knew it, and George did too.

It was not she who had saved him from drowning, it was luck. Luck too that had kept him from crashing his car today. But she had likely prevented his arrest, and there were innumerable small acts of salvation these past six years; how many times had she rolled him on his side, driven or walked him home, explained away his headaches and his absences, watered down his drinks? Sometimes she would fail, and he would look foolish or get dumped by some girl or have to make a round of apologies. Those were the closest calls between V-J Day, when she had been afraid to indict herself, and today, when she realized she was perhaps more afraid of being a bad sister than a bad mother. The first responsibility was entrenched by now, the second still new. Or maybe George was her favorite.

She would not have more children. It would be no trouble making the case to Arthur Senior; they could focus on the one, give him everything they had. The thought provoked a swell of guilt, but after that subsided, what remained was all relief.

George forgot he'd told Leah he would watch the baby. She had called the night before, Friday, not quite dinnertime, and he wasn't sure what he would do with himself that June evening. There were a couple of girls he might yet call.

Leah wanted to remind him about the birthday party Sunday, she said. She checked in a few times a week, always with some pretense. She probably knew he saw through her.

He was well into cocktail hour, listening to his sister tell him she still had a lot to do and that Arthur Senior would likely end up back at the office tomorrow, and so to cut her off—maybe he would call one of these girls, best do it now—he said, "I'll watch the baby."

She said nothing.

"So you can go to the bakery and all of that."

Leah was reluctant—he knew it, and she knew he knew—but she agreed. He would come at one; she wouldn't be out long. "All right, George? One o'clock?"

They hung up, and he called the girl who would become his first wife. No answer, so he called the other girl.

Out that evening, they ran into Dolly, who was with a couple of girlfriends. Dolly would be dead of cancer within twenty years, during which time she and George kept a wary, unspoken peace. Many times she tried to speak of it, to what end he could never precisely say. Something to do with her own magnanimity. That night he caught her eye and held up a hand. She nodded, and he watched her take in the girl he was with, her lovely profile, then the swivel of her lovely neck to make polite acknowledgment.

On Saturday George poured his first drink at 11 a.m., and Leah called at 1:15. "I just want to know if you're actually coming, because—"

"I'm on my way!" He put his tumbler in the sink, drank a large glass of water, brushed his teeth, and drove the few blocks.

When his sister left, he downed three tidy drinks made with her good liquor, then lay on the floor beside Arthur Junior's playpen. The baby banged his toys and gibbered, and George tried not to doze. He slapped his cheeks, he sang a little, he drummed his feet. Eventually he decided to put Arthur Junior in the car. The baby would be lulled, and George would perk up with something to concentrate on. They could come back in fifteen or twenty minutes and both have a nap.

When Leah told him what happened, George swallowed his shock. He remembered getting in the car with his nephew, settling him in the seat he'd lifted from its hook in the entryway, then waking up in his own apartment. Leah called to say that what she wanted right now was to get through the birthday party. "So straighten up," she told him, "and come when you're expected." They would have it out later.

They never did. But she locked the liquor cabinet and maneuvered so George wouldn't ever be alone with Arthur Junior; he didn't let on that he noticed any of it. She still saved him in all the small ways he required, but in the one other instance he'd dodged arrest he was alone. It was ten years on, still decades before the phenomenon of drunk driving would take hold, culturally and legally, and he ended up with only a ticket.

Leah had hardly ever mentioned the time he could have killed her son, and she never labeled it so starkly. But their whole lives she had talked about fearing George drowned. He might not otherwise recall it. It was stupid to get drunk and swim by oneself, but everyone had teenage skin-of-the-teeth stories. He had a good handful more. Youth was dangerous.

Certainly her terror had been sustained, minutes upon minutes—an hour? longer?—of believing him dead, and this he understood as a primary reason that finding them at the quarry had been so much less searing. But nothing had happened! Nothing had ever happened, only close calls and minor scrapes, and yet for decades she had behaved as though losing him in the lake were the story of her life, or at least its beginning. Could he have absolved her? Would he?

Her saving him had been convenient. Maybe he'd be dead otherwise. Or maybe he was only lazy and self-indulgent and willing to let someone else answer for him. Maybe that was the final estimation. Maybe it was the story of his life.

* * *

Two days after blacking out under the portico, when George had spent nights under observation and been made to understand he'd had a seizure and then a concussion, Arthur Junior brought him home. He was installed on the couch, and his nephew sat down opposite.

"How do you feel?" Arthur Junior asked.

George exhaled. He felt okay, but he was tired of talking about it.

"I'll stay a bit and make sure you're settled."

"Thank you."

He would have to see the doctor again, but they didn't know what was wrong with him. Old people could have seizures for any number of reasons, but whatever it was he shouldn't drink for a while. He guessed Arthur Junior had already been by to clear out his wine.

They didn't talk for a minute, and George drifted until his nephew said, "I have your money."

He had almost hoped it were gone. It was evidence, nearly as embarrassing to be discovered with so many bills as with pot itself.

Arthur Junior took out his wallet and counted. "Here. $500."

"Who found it?" George took the money and set it on the coffee table between them.

"I don't know. Dad gave it to me. A nurse or somebody gave it to him."

"It's all there." He was surprised to have the full amount back and felt a stab of guilt for that.

"I am glad to hear it."

George calculated a moment and decided a bit of the truth would make him look ridiculous but forthcoming, and no one would suspect the full truth. "I wanted to give it to the college students," he said. "Our two students, your dad's and mine."

"Hmm," Arthur Junior said. "Do you still want to?"

George considered before answering. "I guess not."

They were quiet again. "I've been saving," he offered. "It adds up."

Arthur Junior uncrossed his legs and leaned forward. "Did they ask you for money?"

"No no!" The last thing George wanted to do was impugn the students. *Oh shame.* "No, Art. They're nice kids, and students are always poor, and I had the money. . ." *Oh lies. Oh shame.*

His nephew sat back. "George, I have to tell you—"

"Where does it come from? My hundred per week?"

Arthur Junior lifted one hand, waving off the question, and looked out the window. George waited several seconds, then cleared his throat to relieve the heavy silence. "I want you to take it. You can keep it for me."

Arthur Junior was slow to pull his attention back. His voice was low when he spoke. "George, it's meant for you."

"I know." Oh dear nephew, Leah's boy. "Hold it for me. Please. You'll be doing me a favor."

Arthur Junior studied him, and George went on. "I still have some, for my incidentals. Give this back—" he pointed at the $500—"at fifty per week." It should probably be less since he wasn't supposed to drink. "Otherwise, I'll end up doing something else foolish with it."

A smile started at one side of Arthur Junior's mouth. He reached for the money and set it on his knee. "Do you have an envelope?"

"Dollars are dollars, Art. Put it back in your wallet. You'll remember $500."

"All right," he said, and George watched him do it.

"Now George, I have to tell you." He touched two fingers to his eyebrow. "Mom died. It was early this morning."

George noticed his own inhalation, the very next one, as though it were something newly switched on. "He relented?"

"Yes."

"It's good, isn't it?"

"Yes. It's good. I don't think she was in pain, but—" Arthur Junior looked toward the window again.

"How would we know?"

George wished he hadn't said that, though his nephew barely winced. "We wouldn't," he answered. "But chances are."

"How is your dad?"

"He's got something to help him sleep."

George looked where Arthur Junior was looking, at the yellow-green of April, at nothing. Of course Arthur Senior couldn't keep her alive forever, but he'd tried, and they'd had weeks enough of waiting that George had almost gotten used to seeing Leah the way he had the last time—when was it? three days ago?

"Art? I don't want to be like that."

"I know." His nephew's eyes were on him. "I didn't think Dad would dig in this way. But I will be in charge for you. Remember?"

He didn't, but it was a relief. "How are you, Art?"

"I'm okay. How are you?"

George thought for a few seconds. "I don't know."

"It is strange."

"Did your dad say anything about the money?"

"I don't think it quite registered, George."

He heard the careful patience in Arthur Junior's voice. "I loved Leah," George said. "You know she saved me. Over and over again."

"I know."

"I am sorry. About your lovely mother."

"Thank you. Me too."

"It's going to happen to all of us."

"Yes."

"Can you believe it?"

"Not really."

George remembered he'd had a seizure, and he wondered if he would have another one. He would know what it was this time.

"She saved me," he said again.

"I know it, George. I am glad she did, and I will still come to visit you, and Dad too."

Well, what if she hadn't? It wouldn't matter much to anyone. Arthur Junior would have one less worry. This wasn't self-pity; it was the plain truth. His nephew and his brother-in-law were kind and dutiful, and George's loyalty to them was like an oath, but he had stayed saved all these decades for Leah only. His loyalty to her was like a creed.

A galloping realization moved more quickly then through his body than it could through his mind, and there was a cracking-open sensation in his chest that gave him a jolt of terror so quick it was already past when he noted it. By then it had become elation.

He wished he hadn't told Arthur Junior to decrease his allowance, and there would be no weekly bottles from him either. But he'd have his fifty, and he still had several hundred in the drawer. He would be secretive. He wouldn't embarrass Arthur Senior or obligate Arthur Junior. He would buy very cheap and stockpile when he could and join the Saturday trips to the store as well as the Wednesday ones.

He'd had a seizure, but he was eighty-seven and he would or he wouldn't have another one. From here on to the end, it wouldn't matter what he did because he had stayed saved just as long as he'd needed to. *Oh lovely Leah!* What more could be required of him? It was the major accomplishment of his life.

ACKNOWLEDGMENTS

I am grateful to the journals where these stories first appeared: "When My Father Was in Prison," *Indiana Review*, *The Drum*, and *Midwestern Gothic*; "The Entomologist," *Alaska Quarterly Review* and *Sequestrum*; "Mother and Child," *Witness*; "With You or Without You," *Confrontation*; "Baby True Tot," *Quarter After Eight*; "Ordinary Circumstances," *McSweeney's*; "Last Things," *december*; "Not Dead Yet," *Anomaly*; "Seeing Leah," *Day One*.

Many thanks are due. To Autumn House Press for giving these stories book form, and to Dana Johnson for seeing something in them. To the Association of Writers & Writing Programs' Writer to Writer Mentorship Program, most especially to Christine Sneed for her guidance and encouragement that have stretched across years now. To the MFA Program for Writers at Warren Wilson College and my generous and brilliant teachers, Maud Casey, C. J. Hribal, Erin McGraw, Michael Parker, and Steven Schwartz. To reading and writing friends, particularly Lisa Van Orman Hadley, Jennifer Wisner Kelly, Mary Medlin, and Lenore Myka. To my parents, Mary Moore and Bill Moore, for early exposure to books, and to them and my grandfather, Edmund Knaffle, brother, Spencer Moore, and niece, Willa Moore, for sustained encouragement.

And most of all to my husband, Dustin Morris, first reader and chief enthusiast, all my love and thanks.

HADLEY MOORE's fiction has appeared in *McSweeney's Quarterly Concern*, *Witness*, Amazon's *Day One*, *Alaska Quarterly Review*, the revived *december*, *Indiana Review*, *Anomaly*, *Quarter After Eight*, *Confrontation*, *The Drum*, *Midwestern Gothic*, and elsewhere. She is an alumna of the MFA Program for Writers at Warren Wilson College and lives near Kalamazoo, Michigan.

NEW AND FORTHCOMING RELEASES

Cage of Lit Glass by Charles Kell

WINNER OF THE 2018 AUTUMN HOUSE POETRY PRIZE, SELECTED BY KIMIKO HAHN

Not Dead Yet and Other Stories by Hadley Moore

WINNER OF THE 2018 AUTUMN HOUSE FICTION PRIZE, SELECTED BY DANA JOHNSON

Limited by Body Habitus: An American Fat Story by Jennifer Renee Blevins

WINNER OF THE 2018 AUTUMN HOUSE NONFICTION PRIZE,
SELECTED BY DAISY HERNÁNDEZ

Belief Is Its Own Kind of Truth, Maybe by Lori Jakiela

Epithalamia by Erinn Batykefer

WINNER OF THE 2018 AUTUMN HOUSE CHAPBOOK PRIZE,
SELECTED BY GERRY LAFEMINA

Praise Song for My Children: New and Selected Poems
by Patricia Jabbeh Wesley

Heartland Calamitous by Michael Credico

Voice Message by Katherine Barrett Swett

WINNER OF THE 2019 DONALD JUSTICE POETRY PRIZE, SELECTED BY ERICA DAWSON

The Gutter Spread Guide to Prayer by Eric Tran

WINNER OF THE 2019 RISING WRITER PRIZE, SELECTED BY STACEY WAITE

For our full catalog please visit: http://www.autumnhouse.org